MURDER AT THE BOAT CLUB

A GINGER GOLD MYSTERY # 9

LEE STRAUSS

la plume
PRESS

COPYRIGHT

La Plume Press

3205-415 Commonwealth Road

Kelowna, BC, Canada

V4V 2M4

www.laplumepress.com

Library and Archives Canada Cataloguing in Publication Title: Murder at the boat club : a cozy 1920s murder mystery / Lee Strauss. Names: Strauss, Lee (Novelist), author. Series: Strauss, Lee (Novelist). Ginger Gold mystery. Description: Series statement: A Ginger Gold mystery ; 9 Identifiers: Canadiana (print)

20190107707 | Canadiana (ebook) 20190107715 | ISBN 9781774090251 (hardcover) | ISBN 9781774090268 (softcover) | ISBN 9781774090275 (IngramSpark softcover) | ISBN 9781988677965 (EPUB) | ISBN 9781774090206 (Kindle) Classification: LCC PS8637.T739 M87 2019 | DDC C813/.6—dc23

ISBN: 978-1-77409-026-8

GINGER GOLD MYSTERIES

(IN ORDER)

CHAPTER ONE

*O*ne never knew what might happen at a boat race, but Mrs. Ginger Reed—the former Lady Gold—hadn't expected murder.

Such unseemliness also did not occur to the other spectators currently enjoying the final moments of the boat race between the University of London and the University of Leeds.

The teams were neck and neck approaching Chiswick Bridge. Long boats shot through the water with the powerful strokes of the eight oarsmen sculling with a single oar each; the shouts of the coxswains huddled in the sterns of the boats reverberating over the waters of the Thames, magnified by leather megaphones.

Ginger and her new husband, Chief Inspector Basil Reed, were there to cheer on the London team, not only because they were Londoners, but because the young man rowing in position number six was the son of Basil's good friends the Honourable Thurston Edgerton and his wife, Mrs. Beatrice Edgerton. The two couples stood together along the rail of the University of London Boat Club.

Thurston Edgerton, a tall, barrel-chested man, had a commanding presence and his voice bellowed out the name of his son. "Come on, Garrett!"

Mrs. Edgerton was his visual opposite, rail-thin and tight-lipped. She held with a firm grip on to the wooden railing.

Ginger clung to Basil's arm. "Darling, this is so exciting!"

Though not as famous and as well attended as the annual Boat Race between Oxford and Cambridge, this race was a great event for Ginger, who had been informed that all forms of boat racing were popular amongst the English.

As the boats approached the finish line, the roar of the crowd swelled. Ginger's heartbeat hammered in her chest. It was such a thrill to see young men in fine form working together as if one beast, toward a common goal. She couldn't refrain from shouting encouragement herself.

"Come on, London!"

When London pulled across the finish line only

inches ahead of Leeds, Ginger threw herself into Basil's arms. "They did it!"

"Yes, they did!"

Thurston and Beatrice Edgerton were less demonstrative, being thoroughly British, Ginger supposed. It was at times like this that Ginger found difficulty in keeping her American upbringing in check.

Basil and Mr. Edgerton shared congratulatory handshakes.

Mrs. Edgerton showed a faint blush across her pale cheeks. "Considering Garrett was a late entry to the team, he did very well, did he not?"

"He did indeed," Ginger said. "Congratulations!"

They watched their team accept the trophy, all of them holding back wide grins, then slapping each other on the back as soon as their formal rank broke up. Eventually they returned to the boat club to shower and change. They couldn't possibly join the festivities being held in their honour wearing their team kit of white shorts and purple vests.

Mrs. Edgerton had taken it upon herself, with the permission of the boat club, to host the postrace party, and she disappeared inside the boat club building to oversee the preparations.

Having never attended a boat race, Ginger had been uncertain as to what to wear, and choosing the right outfit was, as far as she was concerned, as important as the event itself. In the end, she'd settled on a tunic-and-skirt outfit of blue and white crepe de Chine. The jumper was elaborately encrusted with tiny seed pearls in stylised waves, fitting for a water-themed function. A snug cloche hat covered all but two red curls which landed nicely on her cheeks. Flesh-coloured silk stockings did help to keep her legs warm against the breeze floating off the river.

Ginger hooked her arm through her husband's as they ventured inside the boat club.

"That was jolly good fun."

"Rather good fortune that the University of London team won," Basil said. "By the look on Beatrice's face," he added under his breath, as the lady in question was approaching, "one would think their son had won the race single-handedly."

Basil had informed Ginger earlier that the Edgertons' son, Garrett, had been a reserve for his team, and wasn't even meant to race. Another oarsman's misfortune had given the young man his opportunity.

Mrs. Edgerton greeted each person she encountered with cheer as she made her way to Ginger and Basil. She wore an Atelier Bachroitz, a designer Ginger admired, and the frock was perfect for the outdoor sporting event, Ginger thought, and mirroring her own outfit.

The three-storey boathouse had a charming, rustic

feel with bark open-wood beams against a mix of white plaster walls and contrasting wood panelling. The ground level, where the boats and equipment were stored, had wide wooden doors that opened toward the Thames, and in the attic above, Ginger had been told, were a few small bedrooms. A fire roared in a vast stone fireplace in the open meeting room, which was furnished with various mismatched armchairs and settees. French windows opened onto a railed-in balcony overlooking the river.

Ginger spotted her sister-in-law and grandmother by her first marriage in attendance. The Dowager Lady Gold occupied one of the chairs. Ginger was becoming used to the elder lady's recent hairdo. No longer fashioned in a Victorian top-of-the-head bun, her grey hair was styled in short, sleek Marcel waves. She sat upright and leaned on her silver-handled walking stick as if she might catch something dreadful if she allowed herself to relax. Standing beside her was a trim and very modern Felicia Gold who defied the cold by wearing a day frock with a sailboat collar that exposed her clavicles. A navy-blue cloche hat topped her auburn bob, and her delightful grey-blue eyes seemed to scan the room to take in the numerous youthful and virile young men sportily dressed. Ambrosia's lined face tensed around her mouth in obvious annoyance.

Ginger knew her grandmother-in-law very well,

and the elderly lady had little patience for what she considered to be flippant fanfare. She'd agreed to join them only because she believed members of the peerage would attend the celebration. Unfortunately, none of her class, apart from the Edgertons, had yet to enter the club.

A waiter arrived with the champagne, and Ginger and Basil graciously accepted. They stepped in beside their hosts.

Mr. Edgerton announced, "I'm so proud, I feel like I might burst a button."

"Deservedly so," Basil said.

Thurston Edgerton pulled Basil aside leaving Ginger alone with their hostess.

"Your efforts appear to be delightfully successful, Mrs. Edgerton," Ginger said. "There's a tremendous amount of excitement in this clubhouse."

"The boat race brings its own excitement, Mrs. Reed."

"It was rather thrilling, especially near the end. I confess to never having attended one before."

Mrs. Edgerton's sharp brows inched up. "It's impossible to be British and not to have been to a boat race. The sport has reigned from ancient times."

"I'm thankful to have had the opportunity and fulfilled my duty as a British citizen."

To Ginger's delight, her good friends the vicar of

St. George's Church, Reverend Oliver Hill, and his wife, Matilda, came into view. She excused herself and greeted them warmly.

"Oliver! Matilda! I didn't see you at the race."

"Well, with such a thick crowd," Oliver said cheerily, "it's not a wonder."

Oliver and Matilda were newlyweds as well, married only a couple of months before Basil and Ginger. Matilda's rounded girth proclaimed the child they soon expected. Even though Ginger was sincerely happy for them, she couldn't help but feel a sense of personal loss. Every time she saw Matilda, she felt a pang at the reminder she was unable to conceive herself. Well-rehearsed at hiding those emotions, Ginger pushed the thoughts firmly to the back of her mind.

"Ginger," Oliver said. A tall, wiry man in his thirties, Oliver possessed hair as red as Ginger's and a good number of freckles around a ready smile. "I didn't know you were a fan of the sport."

"Basil is good friends with the Honorable Thurston Edgerton and his wife," Ginger explained. "Their son Garrett rowed for the University of London."

"That's right," Oliver said. "I heard they'd offered to arrange this reception."

Matilda added, "So lovely it turned out to be a celebration."

"Bernard Ramsey is one of our parishioners," Oliver said. He nodded to a table of sandwiches and appetizers being enjoyed by several of the oarsmen who wore trousers, club blazers, and purple team scarves draped around their necks. "The fellow with curly hair. He's number eight. We came to support him and all the oarsmen. I used to row for my college. Number eight as well."

Basil had explained to Ginger how each oarsman was assigned a number that corresponded to the order they sat in the boat. Ginger had been fascinated that they worked as one beast, backs to the finish line as the small coxswain shouted at them through a megaphone from the stern.

Oliver and Matilda excused themselves to mingle, and moved about in their exercised, genial manner. Mrs. Edgerton had circled around, a fresh glass of champagne in her hand.

Ginger watched Mrs. Edgerton's eyes steady on the group of young men, and on Garrett Edgerton in particular, who, unlike his team-mates, held nothing to eat or drink in his hand. Mrs. Edgerton lowered her voice in confidence. "Garrett wasn't even supposed to race today. Apparently, one of the oarsmen got a little too friendly with the coach's wife, or was it the other way around? Regardless, his lack of judgement brought luck to my son."

Ginger held back her shock. She'd learned that an oarsman had left the team, but Basil hadn't mentioned it was due to scandalous reasons. Perhaps he hadn't known. Mrs. Edgerton would be appalled in the morning at how loose her lips had become after one too many drinks.

Ginger's attention was drawn to the sound of angry voices, and as she looked over, she saw Garrett pull back his hand as if he was having to make a real effort not to punch the curly-haired oarsman confronting him. Ginger held in her alarm as she recognised the antagonist as the Hills' friend Mr. Ramsey. Garrett tugged on his blazer and sensibly walked away, and thankfully, the situation was defused.

Mrs. Edgerton went on, oblivious to the drama. "I admire Mr. Ainsley's decisiveness, though one does wonder if he punished his wife for her indiscretions as well. Oh, speak of the fox in the briar."

Ginger followed Mrs. Edgerton's gaze to the handsome couple entering the club. A young, well-dressed lady with hair nearly the same red tone as Ginger's linked arms with an older man in white trousers and the same club blazer and scarf as the team members he coached.

"That's Mr. and Mrs. Ainsley," Beatrice said under her breath. "He's the coach. She looks rather a lot like you, Mrs. Reed, though I'm sure that's where the comparisons stop. There are at least twenty-five years between them, not that that's worth mentioning, except for the fact that she has a taste for young men. Younger than herself."

The sharp edge of disapproval wasn't softened by her whisper. As the couple drew nearer, it appeared as if Beatrice Edgerton's sense of propriety overrode her reproach.

"Mr. Ainsley, Mrs. Ainsley," she said, feigning a smile. "Congratulations! Such a spectacular win for our team."

Mr. Ainsley's chest puffed and widened. "I can't say I'm surprised. My young men know how to work hard."

"I'm just pleased that Garrett could be a part of it." Beatrice smirked at the coach's young wife, an acknowledgment that it was Carol Ainsley's indiscretions that had given her son the opportunity. She shot Ginger a look then remembered her manners. "Oh, forgive my rudeness. Here I am gushing about you and your team, Mr. Ainsley, and I've forgotten to introduce you to Mrs. Reed. She's married to Chief Inspector Reed, a friend of my husband's."

Ginger held out her gloved hand. "How do you do? It's a pleasure to meet you both."

"It's our pleasure to meet you too," the coach said. "Ah, Edgerton!"

Garrett Edgerton had drawn into their circle. On closer inspection, Ginger observed that the younger Mr. Edgerton was indeed handsome with a sturdy build and a ready smile. Like the other rowers, he wore the team kit which included the purple scarf, monogramed with the letters *GE*. His right wrist was bandaged but obviously not damaged enough to keep him from rowing, and Ginger wondered if his injury signified a bad temper. Beyond that, she thought the young man appeared a mite pale.

Mr. Ainsley patted Garrett on the back with three firm slaps. "Good job, number six. Not bad for your first race."

Garrett's lips tugged up at the praise. "Thanks, sir."

A brief look passed between Carol Ainsley and Garrett Edgerton before the former pulled on her husband's arm. "I'm dying for a glass of champagne."

"Yes, well," Mr. Ainsley said. Then to Ginger and Mrs. Edgerton, "Please excuse us. We've plenty of people to greet."

"Of course," Ginger said amiably.

Ginger noted Garrett's lingering gaze as the couple walked away and disappeared into the crowd.

"Garrett only just made the team this year due to unforeseen circumstances," Thurston Edgerton said as he stepped into their circle. "I told Beatrice she's overdoing it with this production, but since when did she ever listen to me?"

"Oh, Thurston, please don't bicker in front of our guests," Mrs. Edgerton said. To Ginger, she added, "He's always such a spoilsport. Garrett was ill when the season first started, with bronchitis, which was why he didn't get selected for the team. He couldn't help the fact he wasn't well. Bad timing, I say, and fate has corrected the error. Call it poetic justice, if you will."

"Mum, you're too much," Garrett said with a stiff grin. He coughed into his fist, and Ginger hoped his illness was indeed a thing of the past. She noticed that the young man's attention had wandered and his gaze kept flitting over her shoulder. She turned to see what the source of his distraction was and couldn't keep a grin from pulling up her lips when she saw it was Felicia.

"That lovely young lady is my sister-in-law," Ginger said, gaining the lad's interest. "Would you like me to introduce you?"

Garrett chuckled. "Yes, please."

CHAPTER TWO

Ginger thought Garrett Edgerton was a bit too saucy for his own good, but his grandfather was an earl so Ambrosia would be sure to approve. Felicia could do worse, and Ginger was a little worried that she might do that. Felicia wasn't known for her good judgement, especially when it came to potential love interests.

Felicia stood near the beverage table with a glass of champagne at her lips when Ginger approached with Garrett at her side.

"Felicia, darling?"

On hearing Ginger's voice, Felicia turned, "Ginger, how long is this dreary—oh." She turned on the charm when Garrett came into view. "Never mind. Things seem to be livening up."

Ginger chastised Felicia with a strong look. Her

former sister-in-law was indeed one of those bright young things who didn't quite know what was meant by decorum.

"Felicia, this is Mr. Garrett Edgerton, son of Basil's good friend, the Honourable Thurston Edgerton, and as you already know, an oarsman on the University of London team. Mr. Edgerton, I'm pleased to introduce you to Miss Gold."

Garrett Edgerton held out his hand, and Felicia placed her lace-gloved hand into it.

"It's a pleasure, Miss Gold."

"Likewise, Mr. Edgerton. Such a display today! Congratulations on your magnificent win!"

"Thank you, Miss Gold. It certainly made my day."

Felicia giggled and held up her champagne. "Would you like to join me in a glass?"

"I'd be delighted."

Ginger left the two of them to get to know each other and mingled with the other guests. A boxy woman with an ample bosom fell into step with her. The current fashion of straight-cut boyish styles, unfortunately, didn't do her type of figure any favours. She looked rather like she wore a small tent made of silk and crepe de Chine. Her hat housed a flamboyant collection of peacock feathers.

"You must be the new Mrs. Reed," she said. "I'm Mrs. Pritchard."

"Pleased to meet you, Mrs. Pritchard. Are you acquainted with my husband?"

"I know him only by reputation. My son, Howard, is the captain of the University of London rowing team." Mrs. Pritchard's eyes sparkled with admiration as she pointed. "He's the one with dark hair parted in the middle. All the young men look up to him."

Howard Pritchard was a rugged-looking young man with a flat nose that might have been broken once or twice. Ginger wondered about the oarsman's temper. Or perhaps he practiced boxing as another sport?

"You must be very proud."

"I am. Now some of the other young men should look to his example. Apparently, there's some ungentlemanly carousing, if you know what I mean."

"Is that so?" Ginger wondered if that was what the tense exchange between the rowers had been about.

"Well—" Mrs. Pritchard's next foray into gossip was stopped by Ginger's grandmother-in-law entering the area.

"There you are!" Ambrosia said as she strutted over using the silver-topped cane with her bejewelled hand.

"Grandmama, do you know Mrs. Pritchard? Her son is the captain of the team we rooted for today."

Ambrosia stared at Mrs. Pritchard over the rim of

her glasses, and Ginger felt a twinge of pity as the lady seemed to shrink under the scrutiny.

"Lady Gold," Mrs. Pritchard said with a slight curtsy.

"Good afternoon, Mrs. Pritchard." To Ginger, she added, "We've met, of course. The Pritchard family is well established."

"The Gold family is renowned, of course," Mrs. Pritchard added politely. She lifted a fleshy arm to wave down her offspring. "Oh, Howard!" To the Gold ladies, she said, "I haven't had a chance to congratulate my son. Again, it's been a pleasure, Lady Gold."

"That woman is an insufferable gossip," Ambrosia said once the offending person had stepped away.

"Not that we've never been guilty of such vice."

"Oh, Ginger, please do stop," Ambrosia muttered. "I don't suppose you can summon Clement? I knew it was a mistake to come with Basil. Now we're trapped here until he's ready to go. I really don't know why I talked you into dragging me along. I believe I have sand in my hair."

Ginger couldn't help but chuckle a little. "You don't have sand in your hair, Grandmother. We weren't anywhere near the embankment. Admit it. You found the race at least a little thrilling, didn't you?"

"I'm not sure thrilling is a good thing at my age."

Ambrosia's expression tightened. "Oh, my word, with whom is Felicia speaking?"

Ginger followed Ambrosia's gaze. "That is Mr. Garrett Edgerton, one of the University of London oarsmen."

"Edgerton? His father is the Honourable Thurston Edgerton?"

"That's true."

Ambrosia's demeanour brightened. "Well, this is marvellous! I was so concerned that Felicia would fall in with a bad crowd, but the Edgertons are a good family. Good bloodlines can't be taught."

Ginger rolled her eyes. "He's only talking to her, not proposing."

"One must certainly precede the other, Ginger, and they're both of an age where they're looking at matrimonial prospects."

Ginger didn't fancy getting into a sparring match with Ambrosia. "I'm sure you're right, Grandmother. Now if you'll please excuse me."

Ginger felt it was time to return to Basil and spotted him on the other side of the room. She passed behind the doe-eyed Felicia and the flirtatious Garrett, who peered out of the boathouse to the river below where some of the other oarsmen were gathered.

Ginger overheard Felicia ask, "Who is the tall one on the left with blond hair?"

"That's Miles Brassey," Garrett replied. "He's stroke. Or," he added with a smirk, "number two, as we like to call him, but he doesn't appreciate the handle."

Felicia laughed. "I imagine not."

Ginger reached Basil's side and said lightly, "I think Felicia has an admirer."

"Garrett Edgerton?" Basil asked.

"Yes. What do you think? Do you approve?"

Ginger was perplexed to see Basil's brows furrow.

"Edgerton says the lad is troubled. Maybe more than Felicia could manage."

"Oh mercy," Ginger said. "Don't tell Ambrosia that. She's already planning the wedding."

Ginger couldn't hear what was being said between Felicia and young Mr. Edgerton, but one moment Felicia laughed at something he said, and in the next, her champagne flute slipped from her hand. The glass shattered at Felicia's feet just as Garrett Edgerton crumpled to the ground.

CHAPTER THREE

*E*ven when not scheduled to work at Scotland
Yard, Basil's senses were always attuned to
his surroundings. Even in a relaxed posture, sitting in
an armchair holding a drink casually in one hand, he
was alert. It was a habit long instilled and not easily
broken. When the sound of a lady's voice—Felicia's—
now pitched high, resounded through the rafters of the
boathouse, he set his drink down and jumped to his
feet.

"Garrett? Garrett? *Garrett!*"

A moment of stunned silence fell, followed by
concern, then pure panic.

Basil rushed to the scene. Ginger was already there
with Felicia clutching her arm. Basil, squatting, shook
Garrett's shoulders. When Basil couldn't rouse
Garrett, he lowered his ear to listen for breath. After he

had placed two fingers on Garrett's neck, he shot Ginger a look of distress. He shouted, "Get the doctor!" and immediately began chest compressions.

"Make way! Make way!" Thurston Edgerton pushed through the gawkers to the scene. "Garrett? Stop this nonsense and get up this instant!"

"Thurston!" Beatrice Edgerton's hand covered the bottom half of her face. "Is he all right? Garrett?"

A hum of voices hovered about them as the oarsmen gathered along with the boat club guests. Edgerton bellowed, "Where is the doctor?"

"I'm here. Let me through." A thin man, whose skin hung loosely on his face and who had a bald head that glittered with a sheen of sweat under the electric lighting, arrived. He set his black doctor's bag on the floor. "I'm Doctor Gladstone, team doctor. What happened?"

Basil moved aside so that Dr. Gladstone could examine Garrett's prone form.

"We were just talking," Felicia said. "Leaning against the rail and watching people along the river. It grew chilly outside, so we headed in, and then—"

"Did he seem unwell to you?" Ginger said gently.

"I don't know. Garrett complained about feeling tired, 'dreadfully exhausted', is what he said," Felicia replied. "He coughed rather a lot. I even enquired about his health. This cool dampness can give one a frightful cold if one's not careful. That's what I told him."

"Doctor?" Beatrice said, her voice thin and screechy. "Can you wake him?"

Dr. Gladstone let out a long breath, then slowly shook his head. "I'm afraid he's gone."

Edgerton grew pale and pinched his lips together. Beatrice's eyes fluttered and rolled back into her head. Basil caught her before she hit the ground and laid her there gently.

"Keep an eye on her, please," he said to Ginger, then led Thurston to a chair, saying "Sit here for a moment, old chap." Then in a loud voice, he addressed the room. "I'm Chief Inspector Basil Reed of Scotland Yard. As you are well aware, we have a sudden and unfortunate death. Until we can ascertain the cause of death, please do not leave the premises. Though I ask this of you, politely, as a courtesy for the Edgerton family, it is not actually a request. Thank you for your cooperation."

"Basil?" Ginger said as she drew near his side. "Do you have reason to think Garrett's death suspicious?"

"Not yet, but I don't like to leave any stone unturned. Once in a while, what is deemed to be natural causes turns out to be something more sinister. It's only prudent to take extra care. I've learned that the hard way."

21

Basil shouldered his way through the guests, many of whom had the decency to look away and keep silent.

"Oh, dear Lord," said the lady who Basil had learned was the mother of the stroke oarsman, Howard Pritchard. "I can't imagine my Howard dying out of the blue like that. And in such a public situation. The whole celebration is ruined!"

Howard Pritchard looked abashed by his mother's outburst. "Put a sock in it, Mummy."

Mrs. Pritchard gasped before pinching her lips shut.

"Mr. Brassey," Basil asked of one of the oarsmen. "Direct me to the club's telephone, please." He hoped the boat club was a forward-thinking organisation and had installed the instrument. His worry was short-lived.

"This way, Chief Inspector." Miles Brassey led Basil to a small office area at the back. A black candle-stick-style telephone sat on a large desk. Basil dialled the operator and held the earpiece so he could hear. "Connect me to Scotland Yard, please. It's urgent."

Sergeant Scott answered, an older member of the London Met who had thinning hair and eyes that spoke of seeing more of the dark side of humanity than one would like to admit. Basil trusted him completely.

"Reed here. We have a death at the University of London Boathouse. I need you to bring some men."

"It's suspicious, sir?"

"When a healthy sportsman in his prime suddenly drops dead with only a bit of a cough as a warning, I consider it suspicious."

"We're on our way, sir."

When Basil returned to the room, he found that Beatrice had recovered from her faint and was now sitting rigidly at Garrett's side, sobbing softly into a lace handkerchief. Someone, the doctor perhaps, had found a sheet and covered the body.

"Pritchard," he called to the oarsman he knew to be the captain. "Call your team together. I'd like a word."

Pritchard frowned but nodded. "Yes, sir."

The tension in Basil's shoulders ebbed slightly as Ginger approached.

"Oh, darling," she said, taking his hand. "How awful for your friends. And for you. I'm so sorry this has happened."

"Thank you, love. My heart aches for Edgerton and Beatrice. Garrett was their only child."

Ginger brought her hand to her chest. "Poor things."

His wife's capacity for compassion was one of the many things Basil loved about her. He squeezed her hand in return. Then patted his pockets for his notebook, sighing when he came up empty.

"Are you looking for paper and pencil?" Ginger asked.

"I didn't think I'd need my notebook and left it at home."

Ginger opened her handbag and produced what he needed.

"Now, why isn't it fashionable for men to carry such an apparatus," Basil commented wryly. "One's pockets can't always be counted on."

"Are you going to question the team?" Ginger asked. Her green eyes darted to the group of young men that had collected nearby. "Do you really think Garrett's death is natural?"

"We'll have to wait for an autopsy to know for sure, but it's rather odd for a twenty-one-year-old man in good condition to fall to the floor and die."

"I agree," Ginger said. "I'll mingle with the parents and friends. Maybe they know something that'll shed light."

Basil had full confidence in Ginger's ability to massage pertinent information out of people without them even realising it. He was grateful she was here, especially since it felt like donkey's years since he'd called the Yard.

Approaching the team, he said, "Gentlemen. My condolences on the loss of a chap and team-mate, the turn of what was to be a celebration of a dramatic win.

I realise you must be in shock, but indulge me as I ask a few questions, keeping in mind it's only a matter of form.

"What do you want to know?" Brassey said. He was a cocky chap who stood with legs wide and arms crossed.

"For the record, your names and roles on the team." Basil held the pencil and paper at the ready.

"Howard Pritchard, team captain."

"How long have you known Garrett Edgerton?"

"We attended the same junior school as children."

"So close mates?"

"I wouldn't say that. We've drifted over the years."

There was more Basil would like to ask Pritchard, but it was prudent that he moved on. He shifted his gaze to the next lad. "And you?"

"Horace Lighthouse, sir. I'm seventh. I only met Edgerton a couple of weeks ago when he won Brooks' seat."

"Brooks?" Basil asked.

"Harry Brooks, the chap who got ousted by the coach."

"I see," Basil said as he scribbled down notes with a feeling he would have to get to the bottom of what had happened to this Brooks and the circumstances of his departure.

"Miles Brassey, sir," the next lad said smugly. "I showed you the telephone."

"Yes, I remember. And your position?"

"Stroke, sir."

"And your relationship with the deceased?"

"Like Lighthouse, we only recently met."

Basil had a sinking feeling all the answers regarding Garrett would be similar.

The next two chaps were identical twins. Seeing the exact replicas, side by side, was somehow unnerving.

"We're John and Jerry McMillan," the one on the right said. The fellow on the left added, "Numbers four and five."

Basil scribbled the information down, feeling quite like he was wasting his time. "And only recently acquainted with Mr. Edgerton?"

"Yes, sir," they replied in unison.

Next was a curly-haired chap called Bernard Ramsey. "We have mutual friends," he offered. "Reverend and Mrs. Hill."

"Ah." Basil remembered Ginger mentioning she'd seen them. He glanced about the room. "They're not here any longer?"

"Appears not. Mrs. Hill is in the family way, so perhaps that's why. The doctor says she needs to stay off her feet."

"I see."

The final fellow was the diminutive sort. The top of his head coming to Basil's elbows. "You're the coxswain," he said with an easy guess.

The man nodded. "Jude Fellows, sir. Only knew Edgerton by reputation before he stepped in for Brooks."

"And what kind of reputation was that?"

The young men glanced at each other as an air of apprehension settled.

"Mr. Fellows?" Basil prompted.

"It's just rumours, Chief Inspector. I'd hate to speak ill of the dead."

"I understand. It'll stay in this circle, but it may be vital information."

"For what?" Brassey said. "The bloke had a bad heart or something. Sportsmen drop dead more often than one would like to think."

"True, but again, indulge me. What was Mr. Edgerton's reputation? Heart breaker? Rabble-rouser? Did he drink too much?" Overindulgence in alcohol could've contributed to a weakened physical state."

"Conceit, sir," Jude Fellows finally said. "He was a pompous ass who thought he was better than the rest of us."

. . .

GINGER, satisfied to see Felicia and Ambrosia sitting together—Ambrosia doing her best to provide emotional comfort, but somehow failing—glanced about the rest of the room. Small clusters had formed with middle-aged ladies in one grouping, their male counterparts in another, and a third consisting of the younger university set.

The police arrived, snapped pictures, and took statements. Ginger recognised Sergeant Scott, but a younger, and, she had to admit—her marital status notwithstanding—handsome constable, was new. A second look at Felicia confirmed what Ginger assumed was bound to happen. Her sister-in-law stared at the new officer, her pouty lips parted. She dabbed at the tears around her full, pretty eyes. Poor Garrett, Ginger mused, so quickly forgotten.

Ginger floated into the ladies' circle. "Such a shame," she said.

A collection of hatted heads nodded in agreement. "I can't imagine what poor Beatrice is going through," one of them said.

"She was so proud that he'd *finally* won a seat," said another.

Ginger noted the emphasis on the word, "finally."

"I, for one, think it unfair of the coach to oust Harry Brooks like that," a third woman added.

"Oh?" Ginger said, leaning in as if she enjoyed a

titbit of juicy gossip. "Do you know why he was let go?"

"Some nonsense with the coach's wife is what I heard. Boys will be boys, as they say. It's the coach's problem if he can't rein in his wife."

"I hear she still has a studio from when they were . . . you know."

"Good Lord," exclaimed another.

"When they were what?" Ginger asked.

"Lovers. The coach left his wife for Carol. Getting his comeuppance if you ask me. The first Mrs. Ainsley was a saint, putting up with the way Mr. Ainsley ignored her."

"I heard she got a good sum of money for claiming to be unfaithful so that the courts would grant a divorce, even though she privately insisted she'd never strayed."

Oh mercy. The gossip was indeed juicy, but how did any of that tie in with Garrett Edgerton's death?

"Did any of you know Garrett Edgerton?" Ginger asked.

The stream of words stopped, then the apparent spokeswoman for the group said, "We don't know any of the oarsmen, besides our own sons, that is. Not well, anyway."

"Nor their friends. They come from all parts."

"How do you know each other?"

"Oh, we're members of the bridge club. Though I doubt we'll see Beatrice in attendance any time soon."

Ginger couldn't guess if she'd got any useful information from this lot but filed it away under "just in case". In the same manner that she'd slipped into the group, she slipped out.

Ambrosia sat, back stiff, one hand resting on her walking stick and with a deep frown on her face. The young constable had just moved from asking her questions—Ginger suspected he hadn't got much from her —and now focused on Felicia. Felicia had cleaned up considerably since Ginger had last made note of her: face fresh, lipstick bright red and newly applied, her purple short-brimmed hat pinned neatly on an angle. She stood now, gloved hands folded in front of her lavender wool suit.

Ginger glided just close enough to listen in.

"Hello, Officer."

"Miss, might I have your name?"

"If I can have yours."

Oh mercy, Felicia!

The officer smiled. "I'm Constable Brian Braxton."

Unlike many constables in service of the King, this one had an educated way of speaking. Some joined the police force for reasons other than financial need. Like Basil, for instance.

"I'm Miss Felicia Gold. It's a pleasure."

"Yes, well, I need to ask you a few questions about the deceased Mr. Garrett Edgerton."

Felicia stopped fluttering her eyelashes—thankfully, Ginger thought—and took on an expression appropriately sombre to the occasion. "Of course."

"I understand you were talking to Mr. Edgerton when he died."

"Yes. We were standing just outside." Felicia pointed. "Along the rail. Then we came inside, and then—" she let out a soft sob.

Ginger narrowed her eyes. Felicia was known to be a fine actress, she'd even graced the stage of the Abbott Theatre once, and Ginger couldn't be sure if her performance was real or not.

"I'm sure it's been a big shock, Miss Gold," Constable Braxton said. "How long had you known each other? Were you good friends?"

"Not at all. We'd only met officially at this celebration, though I was aware of him and his part in the race. He's the son of a good friend of my brother-in-law. We came especially to watch him race."

"And your brother-in-law is?"

Ginger couldn't help but smirk. "Chief Inspector Reed."

Constable Braxton looked sincere in his shock. "The Chief Inspector is your brother-in-law?"

"My, you *are* new to town, aren't you?" Felicia said,

her lips twitching in mirth. "He married my sister-in-law, Ginger Gold. Well we're not officially related anymore. Her first husband was my brother. He died in the Great War."

"I'm sorry."

Ginger thought it an excellent time to jump in. "Did I hear my name?"

"Oh, Ginger," Felicia said, reaching for Ginger's hand. "This is Constable Braxton. Constable Braxton, this is Mrs. Reed."

"Pleased to meet you," Ginger said kindly. "I'm so sorry it's under these sad circumstances."

"The pleasure is mine, madam. And yes, I'm sorry too. I understand Mr. Edgerton was a friend of yours?"

"Not mine, so much. I only met the family today. But the Chief Inspector has known the family for a long time."

"Anyway," Felicia said, giving Ginger a subtle nudge. "Constable Braxton was in the middle of questioning me."

"I'm sure I have enough here." The constable took a step sideways and smiled pleasantly. "Good day, ladies."

Once the constable was out of earshot, Ginger arched a brow in question. "Felicia?"

Felicia raised her chin and folded her arms. "What? I was simply doing my duty."

Ambrosia tapped her stick on the wooden floor, capturing their attention. "Can we leave this wretched place now? I need to use the lavatory, and I'm not about to avail myself of facilities shared with a bunch of smelly young men."

CHAPTER FOUR

*W*ith Basil needing to remain behind and oversee the removal of the body, Ginger rang Clement to retrieve her, Ambrosia, and Felicia. A quiet fellow, though entirely competent behind the wheel when performing his duties as a chauffeur, Clement felt more comfortable with his additional tasks keeping the garden and overseeing the garage and stables.

Ginger sat in the front seat of her shiny ivory 1924 Crossley, her new pride and joy. The interior had deep red leather seats and glossy mahogany dashboard trim. She was pleased that Clement had thought to bring her Boston terrier along for the ride.

"Boss!"

The small dog sat on Ginger's lap—stubby tail wagging and tongue hanging, with his wet nose dampening the window. Ambrosia and Felicia rode in the back seat.

Felicia sighed. "It's my fault he's dead."

"Stop being so hysterical, child," Ambrosia said. "You just met the man. How could you be responsible for his death?"

"I'm dashed with bad luck, that's how. Men seem to drop like flies when they attach themselves to me."

Ginger looked over her shoulder. "You'd better stay away from Constable Braxton, then."

"Ginger!" Felicia said.

Ambrosia snapped to attention. "Not that police officer?"

Thankfully, Clement slowed to make the turn down the lane of Mallowan Court in Kensington before the conversation could be taken further.

Ginger's London home was a grand three-storey limestone manor with neatly crafted gardens, thanks primarily to Clement the gardener and all-around handyman. Even so, Ambrosia liked to take a good portion of the credit.

Felicia hurried down the garden path.

Ginger called after her. "Felicia?"

"I just need to be alone!"

"Missus?" On hearing their arrival, Ginger's young ward Scout appeared from the stable. He wore knicker-bockers held up by leather braces, and a newsboy cap.

His blond hair poked out like the straw that clung to his clothes. "Is Miss Gold gonna be alright?" he said, having witnessed Felicia's dramatic departure.

"She will be." Ginger placed a tender palm on Scout's thin shoulder. "A new friend passed away suddenly. She just needs a little time to mourn."

Boss whimpered, and Ginger scooped him into her arms. She nuzzled her nose into his warm fur as she headed for the kitchen entrance.

Ginger had given members of her staff permission to attend the race, including young Scout. They had already been back for some time.

"I 'eard it was an oarsman who kicked the bucket."

"That's a rather crass way of putting it, Scout. Instead, use the term 'passed away.'"

"Sorry, missus." Scout stayed at her side. "What'd 'e pass away of?"

"I don't know."

"But they all looked so strong. 'Ow can a 'ealthy bloke like that just up and kick, er, pass away?"

If the matter at hand hadn't been so serious, Ginger would've reprimanded her young charge for letting his *h's* drop, but now wasn't the time to worry the lad over grammar.

"Most probably a problem that we couldn't see from the outside," Ginger said. "The exertion of the race simply triggered the event."

"What if there's sumfing wrong inside me? Might I suddenly kick the bucket too?"

Ginger stopped. "Oh, Scout." She bent her knees to look the young boy in his blue eyes. Though heading quickly into his teen years, Scout was small for his age, a result of the beggarly conditions he'd lived in when he was on the streets of London throughout the first decade of his life. An orphan, Scout had been raised by an ailing uncle and a misguided older cousin. Ginger had met both Scout and his older cousin Marvin aboard the SS *Rosa* on her journey over the Atlantic from Boston. The cousins had worked in steerage, and Scout had helped to take care of Boss.

Unfortunately, after their uncle had passed away, Marvin had chosen a path of crime and was currently serving time for his bad choices. With Scout alone on the streets, Ginger hadn't wasted a moment thinking about it, before inviting the waif to live with her at Hartigan House. Of course, he had had to come in as a servant, especially since, at the time, Ginger held the title of a baroness, Lady Gold.

But now, as a regular lady without a title or peerage, could Ginger change Scout's position in the home?

The Dowager Lady Gold might put her foot down about that, though technically, she was a guest of Ginger's and not the other way around. Perhaps—

"Can I go now, missus?"

"*May* I go now, and yes, you may."

Scout's short brow wrinkled, clearly not understanding the grammatical distinction, but shot off with his short legs before Ginger could call him back.

Ginger chuckled at the sight.

She entered the house through the back door and stood in the bright morning room where she found the cook.

"Such awful news, Mrs. Reed," Mrs. Beasley said. The older woman was nearly as wide as she was tall and barely fit as she pushed behind the table and chair set. "Clement says the lad was the son of a friend of the chief inspector's?"

"Yes, I'm afraid so."

"Shall I prepare dinner at the scheduled time? Or would you like it sooner now that you're home early?"

Ginger checked her wristwatch. She didn't feel a bit hungry and doubted Felicia did either.

"Let's stay with the appointed time, though I would love a cup of tea now."

Placing Boss on the floor, Ginger headed towards the front of the house. The entrance hall of Hartigan House was striking. An enormous chandelier hung from a high, dramatic ceiling with its lights glittering across the polished black-and-white tiled floor. Tall Areca palms lined the base of a broad, curving staircase that led to the bedrooms on the floor above.

Ginger removed her hat and stole, and seeing Pippins walk her way, she handed the items to her butler. A member of the staff since before Ginger's birth, Clive Pippins was a fixture at Hartigan House. Even though he was now in his seventies, Pippins retained his upright bearing.

"Madam," he said, his cornflower-blue eyes staring softly. "I couldn't help but hear the sad news. My sympathies."

"Thank you, Pippins. It's all such a dreadful shock. So sad for the Edgertons and Garrett himself. He had such a promising future."

"Miss Gold appeared quite distressed."

Ginger wondered at Felicia's ability to suffer a multitude of moods in a single afternoon: joy, shock, allure, blame, and grief.

"Yes, I'll go and see her now. Do you know where she is?"

"I believe she's in the sitting room, madam."

The sitting room could be accessed from the dining room or the entrance hall. Ginger, already in the latter, opened the wooden doors and entered. Waterhouse's *The Mermaid* hung above the mantel. The image of the lovely mermaid combing long red hair reminded Ginger of her mother, with whom she shared a resemblance.

Dejected, Felicia sat in the armchair facing the fireplace, her hat on the floor along with her T-strap shoes. Her dark bob was a mess, and her mascara was smudged under her wide, youthful eyes.

Someone had started the fire, probably Ginger's maid Lizzie, but the drink in Felicia's hand had most likely been retrieved by Felicia herself. The room's drinks' cabinet was always fully stocked. Ginger settled into one of the chairs and put her feet up on the stool. Boss, who'd followed her inside, hopped onto her lap.

"Are you all right, love?" Ginger said.

Felicia let out a soft snort. "Brandy helps."

"It's such a shame," Ginger said. "So young."

"I fancied him, Ginger, that's why he's dead."

Ginger shot Felicia a sharp look. "Don't be silly."

"It's true. Everyone I even become remotely interested in ends up dead, in jail, or suffers some kind of bad luck."

"Perhaps it is true that some of your male friends have encountered unfortunate circumstances, but that's just a twist of fate. It's hardly your fault."

"I think, for the sake of the opposite sex, I'm going to put myself under house arrest. It's the responsible thing to do."

Ginger fought back the grin that threatened to take over her face, and she nodded at the drink in Felicia's hand. "Just how many of those have you had?"

"Only this one. Why? Do you think I'm not serious?"

Ginger couldn't imagine her vivacious sister-in-law staying inside for more than a day, and she didn't dare bring up Constable Braxton's name again. A mite facetiously, she said, "Whatever will you do with your time? That is, when you're not working at the shop."

Felicia raised her porcelain chin defiantly. "I'm going to finish my next book." She leaned forward, her grey eyes bright now with a new determination. "If people are going to die because of me, I'll kill them in my book, instead of in real life."

"You didn't kill anyone," Ginger insisted. "The fact that you met Garrett Edgerton only minutes before his death was just an unfortunate coincidence."

CHAPTER FIVE

*G*inger and Basil rose early the next morning and shared coffee and tea over a breakfast of Mrs. Beasley's astounding kedgeree made with smoked haddock, boiled rice, hardboiled eggs, and curry sauce. Though the flavourful dish offered a brief distraction, the conversation naturally went to the tragic events of the day before.

"How are poor Thurston and Beatrice?" Ginger asked. Though she remained on formal terms with them in person, whilst discussing them with Basil, Ginger reverted to their Christian names.

"They're simply devastated," Basil said after a bite of thickly buttered toast. "Edgerton's in shock. He barely moves a muscle in his face, not even to blink. And poor Beatrice, though she tried to restrain herself, her grief was uncontainable. Their staff scrambled about not knowing what to do."

"How awful," Ginger said with meaning. She knew how heavy and complicated grief was, having lost both her first husband and her beloved father. "Such a hard journey lies ahead."

Basil, also familiar with grief, could only agree.

Ginger adjusted the ruffled opening of her silk rose and lavender negligee which tied loosely at her hips with an attached satin ribbon "Did Garrett have a heart condition?"

"If so, his parents weren't aware of it." Basil wiped his mouth with the cloth napkin. "He was the epitome of good health."

"I thought they said he'd just had bronchitis recently."

"According to Edgerton, Garrett had only suffered from a cold. Beatrice thinks, er—" Basil corrected himself. "*Thought* every chest congestion would lead to bronchitis because Garrett had once been hospitalised with it as a child. But Edgerton was adamant that his son had never been truly sickly since."

"I'm assuming an autopsy shall be done?" Ginger said.

"Indeed. When a young man dies under mysterious circumstances, one must ensure it's not due to an infectious disease."

"Shall Dr. Gupta be performing it?" Dr. Gupta was the city's chief medical examiner and a friend of Ginger's.

"Yes. Edgerton has demanded the best for his son."

The tap, tap of Ambrosia's walking stick on the floor alerted them to her arrival.

"Good morning, Ginger. Basil. I trust you slept well."

"Well enough," Ginger said. "Under the circumstances."

Ambrosia lowered herself into one of the empty chairs. "The circumstances?" Her wrinkled brow collapsed further and then relaxed as memory returned. "Oh, yes. That poor Edgerton fellow. He would've been such a good match for Felicia."

Ginger's jaw dropped. "Grandmother! A man has died, and you think only of Felicia's potential marital loss?"

Ambrosia huffed. "Don't be dramatic, Ginger. One can be saddened by both, can one not?" She stared at Basil. "Please relay my deepest sympathies to the family." She opened her linen napkin and placed it on her lap. "I'll ask Langley to arrange for flowers to be delivered." She reached for the bell sitting on the table and rang it. Soon afterward, Lizzie scurried in and, on seeing Ambrosia, bobbed nervously.

"Fresh tea," Ambrosia said. "And there's no need to

act like a mouse, Lizzie. Goodness knows we have enough of the four-footed kind around here as it is."

Lizzie disappeared behind the swinging door, and Ambrosia stared over her spectacles at Ginger. "The poor thing rather does resemble a mouse, doesn't she?"

After breakfast, Ginger said goodbye to Basil with a lingering kiss before he set off to work at Scotland Yard. Ginger's own dress shop business required her attention, and after spending half an hour in her study on paperwork, she prepared to leave for her Regent Street shop, Feathers & Flair.

Upstairs in her bedroom, Ginger surveyed the day dresses that hung in an ornate wooden wardrobe. The lovely piece matched the bedside tables, a dressing table, and a full-length mirror, along with the delicately etched wooden head and footboard of the bed she now shared with Basil, and Boss, as it were, to Basil's chagrin.

Before she and Basil married, Ginger had updated the decor to include aqua-green walls and plush green and white Persian carpets. Creamy-white pincushion armchairs flanked the windows that were covered in delicate white net curtains

Boss watched her from his spot at the foot of the bed where he sniffed at being awakened from what might've been an exciting dream.

Ginger chose a navy-blue French frock that had

vertical rows of red dots alternating with white. The sleeves were long and narrow, and a white chemise peeked out of a deeply scooped neckline. The matching belt, tied in a bow at her waist, contrasted with the large yellow silk flower pinned to her left shoulder. She paired the outfit with navy pumps and a hat. A quick examination of her figure in the mirror satisfied her. Businesslike, yet fashionably feminine.

Pippins was in the hallway as Ginger passed through on her way to the back garden. "How is Felicia doing?" she asked. "She didn't come down to breakfast, Pippins. Have you seen her yet?"

"I do believe I've heard the sound of typewriter keys being rapidly pounded in the library this morning, madam."

Ginger let out a soft sigh of relief. Felicia was working on another mystery book, which meant she had recovered from her shock the day before. Although Felicia *was* expected to help at the shop today—Ginger employed her precisely to give her sister-in-law something worthwhile to do with her days, not to mention a bit of money of her own—if she was going to keep out of trouble by writing then that would suffice, for now.

The drive to Regent Street was rather uneventful, and Ginger prided herself on not hitting even one kerb, though the potholes on Carriage Drive were harder to dodge. One unfortunate encounter had tossed poor Boss onto the floor.

"Sorry, Bossy."

Feathers & Flair was housed in a two-storey stone structure well situated in the fashion district. Tall windows let in natural light which aided the electric crystal lamps that hung from high ceilings trimmed with gold moulding. The light illuminated the new gowns and frocks displayed on mannequins. Ginger strolled across the polished, white marble floor and greeted her shop manager, Madame Roux.

"Bonjour," Madame Roux said. "Our clients seem delighted with the spring designs, Mrs. Reed."

"Marvellous." Ginger quite liked the new look that had brought in fitted sleeves and slightly higher hemlines.

Madame Roux excused herself to greet a new customer.

Ginger carried Boss across the marble floors, through the velvet burgundy curtain, and commanded him to stay in the dog bed located in the back room. Some of the clientele took exception to a dog being about an expensive dress shop but, Ginger thought, what they didn't know wouldn't hurt them.

She found her dress clerk, Dorothy, and her seamstress, Emma, gossiping about the race.

"I heard it was a kiss of death," Dorothy said as she

pulled new factory-made dresses out of a box, shook them out, and hung them on a rod. "Can't say who the lass was, but he kissed her and then dropped to the floor."

Emma's foot didn't let up on the pedal of the glossy black Singer sewing machine she operated. "She must've been wearing lethal lipstick, eh? That's the stuff of those science fiction shockers."

"But he had a reputation—"

"Ladies," Ginger said.

Both of the young women froze, their gazes snapping to Ginger.

"Sorry, Mrs. Reed," Emma said. "We didn't see you there."

Dorothy wasn't about to be diverted. "It's just talk is that Mr. Edgerton was a ladies' man. They say a lot of girls disliked him because of his ungentlemanly manner."

Oh mercy. And Ginger had practically pushed Felicia into Garrett Edgerton's arms. In the future, she really needed to be more careful with Felicia's heart.

"And you think one of these displeased ladies may have wanted Mr. Edgerton dead?"

"Oh, I don't know, madam," Dorothy said, her eyes growing glassy with distress. "How else does a young man just up and die like that? Oh, forgive me, I shouldn't have spoken ill of the dead. It's just that I'm reading the Freeman Wills Crofts novel, *Inspector French's Greatest Case.* My mind is seeing murder everywhere."

Ginger released the tension that had built up in her shoulders. Dorothy West could be more work than Ginger had bargained for when she employed her, but she hadn't done anything truly awful enough to merit dismissal.

"I suggest both of you stop your gossiping and get to work. Dorothy, I think I heard the bell at the door ringing. Go and see if a new customer needs your assistance."

Ginger spent a couple of hours with customers, and when there was a lull, she helped Dorothy take the new frocks to the upper floor.

Madam Roux's voice reached her from the bottom of the steps. "The telephone rang for you, Mrs. Reed. It's the chief inspector."

"I'll be right down."

Giving Dorothy a look of encouragement to continue working, Ginger made her way down to the main floor and picked up the ornate receiver.

"Basil?"

"Yes, Ginger, it's me. Dr. Gupta rang the Yard and requested that I go and see him."

"Oh mercy," Ginger said. "He must believe foul play is involved if he wants to see you in person."

"I'm afraid so. I just thought I'd let you know so you could prepare Felicia for more bad news."

Ginger had a fleeting thought of a set of lethal lips and was thankful Felicia hadn't kissed Garrett before he died.

CHAPTER SIX

*B*asil disliked the smell he associated with the mortuary. A mix of death, mould, and chlorine with a touch of lemon-scented cleanser. Located in the basement of the University College Hospital on West Moorland Street, the mortuary had limited natural lighting that leaked through small windows where the walls met the ceiling. A large lamp hung low over a white porcelain table situated in the middle of the room. New refrigerated cabinets had been installed along one wall, a much-appreciated advancement to keeping corpses, and their smells, contained whilst waiting for a burial release.

Dr. Manu Gupta greeted Basil as he entered the room.

"Good day, Chief Inspector," Dr. Gupta said warmly.

Basil liked the man who was younger than his predecessor, and more handsome with his caramel-coloured skin and exotic copper-coloured eyes. Basil hadn't needed Ginger to point out that the nurses and female students at the London Medical School for Women were attracted to the pathologist. Unfortunately for them, Dr. Gupta had recently returned from a trip to his homeland of India with a wife on his arm.

Basil tipped his trilby. "Good day, Dr. Gupta."

"I understand you are acquainted with the deceased's parents?" the doctor asked.

"Yes. Thurston Edgerton and I go back a long way. We lost touch for several years, but it's still difficult to watch him suffer like this."

"My condolences all around," Dr. Gupta said.

"Thank you. I understand you have news about the Garrett Edgerton case?"

"Yes, I—"

"Hello!"

Basil pivoted toward the familiar voice that had suddenly interrupted the twosome. "Ginger?" Basil's lips twitched in a slight grin. "How am I not surprised?"

He watched his wife cross the floor as if she owned the mortuary and had somehow transformed it into a fashion walkway.

"Good afternoon, Dr. Gupta," Ginger said pleasantly.

"Hello, Mrs. Reed."

"You don't mind that I dropped in? When Basil rang to let me know you had news about poor Garrett's death, I simply couldn't resist coming."

"I have no problem with you joining us, Mrs. Reed," Dr. Gupta said, "if it's all right with the chief inspector."

"It's quite all right with me, Doctor. What do you know?"

"Garrett Edgerton drowned."

Basil's mind tripped over the pronouncement. He shared a look of astonishment with his wife.

"How is that possible?" Ginger asked. "He wasn't even in the water?"

"It's called secondary drowning," Dr. Gupta explained. "At some point in the last twenty-four to forty-eight hours, Mr. Edgerton had inhaled water. The swelling in the small air sacs in the lungs prevented oxygen from entering the bloodstream. A surprisingly small amount of water can be responsible."

Basil removed a notebook and pencil from his trench coat pocket and scribbled down Dr. Gupta's explanation. Then he said, "So, you're saying he had a near drowning incident in the last two days?"

"Yes," Dr. Gupta nodded.

Ginger nibbled her bottom lip, then asked, "Have you ever seen anything like this before?"

"It's rare," Dr. Gupta said, "and this is the first time I've seen an adult succumb. However, I found scarring in his lungs, which may have weakened his ability to fully remove the water."

"Garrett suffered from a serious case of bronchitis as a child," Basil said.

"What makes you think this is a criminal case?" Ginger asked.

Basil answered for Dr. Gupta. "Garrett was a terrific swimmer. Someone had to have held his head underwater."

"Even after the war," Ginger said indignantly, "I'm still taken aback by mankind's ability to perform heinous acts of violence."

Basil concurred. "It's regrettable."

Ginger tilted her head and smiled at him. "What are the police going to do now?"

"The police shall head to the University of London to interview the rowing team further."

"As it turns out," Ginger said, "I was about to do a little shopping on Kensington High Street. Might I drive with you?"

The way Ginger's mouth curled slightly to one side was proof to Basil that she had invented shopping plans on the spot. Basil had learned long ago that it wasn't worth resisting. Besides, she was often useful and always delightful.

Once they were on their way in Basil's Austin, a 1922 forest-green model 7, he said, "I'm not looking forward to telling Thurston and Beatrice the latest."

"Should we have stopped to see them first?" Ginger asked.

"I'd rather go with some news. Hopefully, we'll gain some information from our interviews."

Ginger twirled a section of her red bob around one finger, an action Basil found quite distracting. He forced his gaze to stay on the road and the horse-drawn carriage he drove by.

The engine of the Austin stuttered, and Basil shifted down in response.

"Is everything all right?" Ginger asked.

"Some kind of hiccup."

"I should have a look later."

Basil admitted to not being mechanically inclined. He knew his wife had learned about automobile mechanics during the war and was quite proficient at keeping her Crossley in tune. Ironic as it was , since her actual driving skills never kept up.

He, luckily or unluckily, had been invalided out of the war early on, so didn't share Ginger's length of wartime experience. It was the reason he'd got into law enforcement. He'd wanted to do his bit somehow. It turned out he was rather good at the job, and even though his social status didn't require it, he stayed on after the war had ended because he desired to do so.

He responded to Ginger, "I'll have to take it into the garage tomorrow."

Ginger hummed in acknowledgment then turned the subject back to the case at hand. "Why would one of the oarsmen attack a fellow team member before the race?"

"We're not talking about a normal man here, love," Basil said. "And remember, Garrett was a reserve. Maybe they didn't know he was going to be standing in for Harry Brooks when the incident happened."

CHAPTER SEVEN

Ginger reminded Basil that it was shorter to get to Kensington from Marylebone if one went through Paddington and cut south through Kensington Gardens rather than circling Hyde Park by way of Mayfair. Ginger had lived in South Kensington for longer, and so it was understandable that Basil mightn't have considered it.

Despite the Austin's engine struggling from time to time, the ride through Kensington Gardens was delightful, with spring-fresh green shoots and leaves on the trees and bushes, and the flower gardens bright with colourful tulips and daffodils.

The Imperial Institute building in South Kensington had been home to the University of London since the year 1900. The impressive Victorian structure had three copper-roofed, Renaissance-style towers. Ginger tapped the head of one of the two stone lions, which flanked the entrance, as they walked in.

The clerk at the information desk acknowledged Ginger and Basil and directed them to a room where Sergeant Scott and Constable Braxton awaited them.

"Chief Inspector," Sergeant Scott said when Basil and Ginger entered and then added with a nod, "Mrs. Reed." Constable Braxton mimicked his greeting.

There had been a time when Basil's team had raised eyebrows and shared furtive glances of disapproval when Basil brought Ginger along on his investigations. After several solved cases which he'd attributed to Ginger's involvement, not to mention the number of times she'd saved his life, the men, for the most part, no longer thought her presence irregular.

"Good day, gentlemen," Basil said. "What do you have so far?"

"We've rounded up five of the seven, plus the cox, sir," Sergeant Scott said. "Mr. Howard Pritchard, the captain of the team; twin brothers, John and Jerry McMillan; and Jude Fellows."

"And the other four?" Basil asked.

"Horace Lighthouse and his cousin Samuel have caught the flu and are under the care of a nurse, Bernard Ramsey is a volunteer at a charity event at his church, and Mr. Brassey has wandered off. We'll round him up, sir."

"Very well," Basil said. "We'll get to them later."

"Oh, let's start with the twins," Ginger said with enthusiasm. "I find twins so fascinating. Especially identical ones. Like oddly exotic bookends."

"Righto," Basil said with a grin.

The McMillan brothers, shorter than the other athletes, shared thick dark hair, hooked noses, and small tight mouths. Strong, well-built arms were obvious under their matching suit jackets and waist-coats, the latter fastened neatly over button-down shirts and stiff collars.

"Mr. McMillan and Mr. McMillan," Basil said. "Please join me in the study room for a quick interview."

This particular room had dark wooden tables, each surrounded by matching wooden chairs and with a Tiffany lamp on one end. The walls were hidden behind rows of book-filled shelves.

Basil removed his coat and hat and hung them on the coat rack by the door. Once everyone sat down, he started the interview.

"If you don't already know, I'm Chief Inspector Reed from Scotland Yard. This is my consultant, Lady Gold."

Ginger and Basil had agreed that it sounded more professional for her to continue to be introduced as Lady Gold, his consultant, rather than as his wife, Mrs.

Reed. Still, the introduction never failed to get looks of disgruntlement or plain distrust. The twins weren't an exception.

Ginger held out a gloved hand. "Of Lady Gold Investigations. It's a pleasure."

The lads hesitantly shook her hand.

One of them spoke for both of them. "Hello. What are we doing here? We don't understand?"

"First, please state your full name," Basil said. "For the record." And so that she and Basil knew which was which, Ginger thought.

The one facing them on the right, the talker, said, "I'm Jerome Mark McMillan."

"And I'm Jonathan Allan McMillan."

Basil made a note. Ginger scribbled something on her notepad as well which she concealed under the table. She showed it to Basil.

John—small scar on the left temple.

Basil glanced at Ginger with a look of appreciation.

"Mr. Garrett Edgerton's death was the result of foul play," Basil said, focusing on the brothers. He and Ginger observed the twins' responses. In an almost synchronised fashion, their eyes widened, and their mouths fell open.

"But how?" John said. "He looked just fine at the party."

Ginger wasn't sure she agreed. In her recollection,

Garrett's complexion was ashen, not just pale from a long sunless winter, and though he tried to hide it, he struggled with his breath, often coughing into his fist.

"We thought he must've had a stroke or something," Jerry said. "It happens to athletes sometimes, even as young as us."

"That was our first thought," Basil said. "However, the medical examiner says otherwise."

"How was he killed, then?" John asked. He looked sincere enough, but Ginger had learned that killers could be terrific actors.

"Where were you fellows the night before the race?" Ginger asked.

"We were on the river, rowing a two-boat," John said.

"Was there anyone who could vouch for that?" Basil asked.

"Well, it was a two-boat," Jerry said. "So just the two of us out on it."

"I can vouch for Jerry," John said.

"And I, John," Jerry recited.

Ginger noted the smug tone that peppered their voices.

"Did anyone else see you?" Basil said, unruffled. "A mate at the boathouse perhaps, or other boaters out?"

John and Jerry glanced at each other. "No," John finally said. "We didn't see anyone."

"Isn't that rather strange?" Ginger said. "Surely other oarsmen were eager to get one last sprint in before the race?"

"It's a long river, milady," John said.

"I don't get what you're playing at," Jerry said, "but it seems like you're looking for an alibi. I don't understand what we were doing the night before the race has to do with the bloke's death on race day."

Basil released the twins, and Constable Braxton ushered Jude Fellows into the room and directed him to take a seat.

Mr. Fellows looked like an ugly child with his short legs that barely reached the floor. Ginger scolded herself for this uncharitable thought. However, what the coxswain lacked in looks and height, he made up for in intelligence.

"I'm a medical student," he said proudly. "I'm too busy with my nose in the books to socialise with the Neanderthals that make up most of the athletic component of this college."

"To be clear," Basil said, "you don't count any of the oarsmen you spend much of your time with as a friend?"

"I'm coxswain because I fit the role, and it gives me certain privileges that, unlike those other boors, I wasn't born with."

"Not everyone is athletic," Ginger said gently. She felt pity for the bitter little man.

"That wasn't the privilege I meant, Lady Gold. I'm speaking about money and elite status. I'm here thanks to a late, but beloved uncle's legacy."

"You didn't like Garrett Edgerton much, I take it," Basil said.

Mr. Fellows eyed Basil with a steely glare, a manner that made Ginger grow cold. "I don't like any of them," he said. "But I didn't kill anyone. I wouldn't be bothered to waste my time. Ten years from now, I'll be a renowned pathologist, and they'll still be playing their balls and hoops."

"You like to work with the dead?" Ginger asked. Her good friend Haley studied that field, and of course, she admired Dr. Gupta's work as well.

"I like to cut things up," Jude Fellows said with a dark glint to his eye.

Ginger released an unreserved shiver when Mr. Fellows left the room. "What a loathsome lad."

"Frightfully unpleasant," Basil said, agreeing, "but he makes a good point. Unless we can find a good motive for him to single Garrett out, he seems to hate everyone equally."

"And there's his size to consider. Could he have held Garrett physically?" Ginger asked.

"Shorter men often compensate for their lack of

height by strength building," Basil said. "I don't think we can rule him out."

"Do you think Garrett knew who attacked him?" Ginger said. "I can't imagine Garrett not seeking retribution, especially if harm came to him at the hands of Mr. Fellows."

"I've thought of that too. Why pretend, as he must've been doing at the boathouse party, to be chums with everyone, if you were aware of your attacker?"

"Unless the person had some kind of hold over Garrett."

"Blackmail?"

"It's possible."

Next to be interviewed was the blond team captain, Miles Brassey, a cocky young upstart with wealthy parents. He slouched in the chair across from Ginger and Basil with legs spread casually and a confident smirk on his face. Miles' eyes often appraised Ginger, and he pulled his lips up in appreciation with each glance.

He thinks himself quite the ladies' man, Ginger thought. She didn't doubt that the young girls flocked to him. He had charm, brawn, and money.

"A lady detective," he said. "I'm amused."

"Then I suppose I've done my job," Ginger quipped. "But perhaps I can entertain you further. Where were you the night before the race?"

Miles' eyes shot to Basil. "You're going to let her do your job?"

"Her job and my job overlap in this instance," Basil said, "but if your hearing improves upon my repeating the question, I shall. Where were you the night before the race?"

Miles snorted. "I was out with friends."

"Which friends might that be?" Basil asked.

"I don't quite remember."

"To clarify," Ginger said, "You don't remember who your friends are? Or you don't have any friends?"

Mr. Brassey sat up indignantly. "I have plenty of friends. I'm a university oarsman. People practically bow when I walk past."

"So, you have admirers," Ginger said. "That's not the same as friends."

"Surely, you must have a good pal?" Basil persisted. "Someone who could confirm your whereabouts and what occupied your time on the night in question."

Mr. Brassey swallowed. "What difference does it make? Edgerton was alive when the race started."

"We have reason to believe foul play caused his death, Mr. Brassey," Basil said.

"What? Is that what this is all about? I had nothing to do with that if it is."

"How did you feel about Harry Brooks getting ousted at the last minute?" Ginger asked.

65

"I think it was a deuced stupid thing for Mr. Ainsley to do," Mr. Brassey said through tight lips. "He let his personal life interfere with our race. Completely inappropriate if you ask me."

"I'm told Mr. Brooks was caught with an illegal substance on his person."

Miles Brassey snorted. "Is that what the coach is claiming? Funny thing, he didn't mind Brooks getting up his wife's skirt."

"Mr. Brassey!" Basil said. "Please do remain civil."

Mr. Brassey shot Ginger a look. "This is why a lady shouldn't be doing a man's job. One always has to bite one's tongue."

Ginger ignored the slight. "Are you suggesting Mrs. Ainsley and Mr. Brooks were involved in an illicit affair?"

"I'm not suggesting it. It's a fact. And he's not the only one, either, but I'm not about to snitch on my mates. The point is, Brooks should have been seven, not Edgerton."

"And now he's not," Basil said.

Mr. Brassey pushed away from the table. "Look here, I'd rather have Brooks on my team than Edgerton, but killing the devil wouldn't put Brooks back on the team. Now, can I go, or do I need to call my solicitor?"

CHAPTER EIGHT

*G*inger had worried about the noises the Austin had been making on their drive from the mortuary to the Imperial Institute building, and now it seemed her concerns were justified. Basil's automobile, parked alongside Eaton Square Gardens, had its green bonnet raised in surrender. Ginger stood beside Basil and stared.

"I'll walk to the nearest phone box and ring for assistance," Basil said.

"Not necessary," Ginger said. "You've got a loose spark-plug wire."

The engine block was the size of a large loaf of bread. In a row along the top, four rubber-encased wires plugged into white sockets. The third one had wiggled loose, which did not stun Ginger considering the rough cobblestoned streets and the potholes.

She peeled off her glove and jemmied the plug until it was once again secure.

"That should solve your problem, good sir," Ginger said playfully.

"This reminds me of the time I found you on the side of the road near Chesterton," Basil said with his eyes flickering with pleasure at the memory. "You were fixing that ancient Coventry Humber with one of your stockings."

Ginger turned and pulled on Basil's lapels. "Were you attracted to me then, Chief Inspector?"

Basil grabbed her by the waist. "Very attracted, Mrs. Reed."

"And I don't intimidate you?" Ginger teased.

"Most men would be intimidated by a woman like you," Basil admitted. He wrapped Ginger with both arms and kissed her. "Good thing I'm not like most men."

Ginger enjoyed these short romantic interludes which were a definite perk to her position as a consultant for Scotland Yard. When she pulled away, she laughed. "We'll have to save some of that for later, Chief Inspector. There's a case to be solved."

It was late afternoon when they finally pulled up to the Edgerton manor in Belgravia. The massive house made Hartigan House look small. A gravel drive circled a large fountain, and Basil parked in front of it.

Ginger pushed the doorbell, which chimed the key notes to Strauss' *Blue Danube.* A few moments passed before the butler answered, predisposed to denying them access.

"Mr. and Mrs. Edgerton are in mourning. They are refusing to see even their closest friends, Chief Inspector."

"I'm very sorry," Basil said kindly. "But I'm afraid it's police business now."

"Police business?"

Basil nodded. "I'm afraid so."

"Very well. Please wait here whilst I announce your arrival."

Basil lifted a palm. "Excuse me, might I use your telephone as I wait."

"Certainly, sir."

Basil followed the butler and Ginger stayed behind.

On one of the walls of the foyer, Ginger noticed a large family photograph taken when Garrett had been about Scout's age. Even though the image was black and white, she could tell his blue eyes sparkled with mischief.

An image of Scout flashed through her mind along with a surprising amount of emotional pain. Not being a parent herself, she'd never identified with this kind of loss before. But Scout. . . If something terrible ever happened to him, she'd be shattered.

Basil returned, interrupting her thoughts.

"I had to report in to Morris before he got too agitated about my '*flittering about with my wife and calling it work.*'"

Ginger chuckled. Superintendent Morris was a difficult man to respect. She and Basil were at best tolerated, and at worst, hindered whenever the super-intendent felt weakened by his own incompetence.

"Ah," Ginger murmured. Her gaze lingered on the family photograph. Taken at an earlier time, the photo-graph showed the elder Edgertons when they were about ten years younger, all of them looking hopeful and happy. "My heart goes out to Mrs. Edgerton," Ginger said. "So hard to lose one's only child."

The butler returned and bowed slightly. "Mr. and Mrs. Edgerton will see you in the sitting room."

The sitting room had the cluttered feel of the late-Victorian era decor with far too much happening on the walls in terms of garish wallpaper and framed photographs. The room was large, but Ginger couldn't imagine another piece of furniture fitting in. Occa-sional tables covered in porcelain ornaments lined the walls, and every chair and sofa had an accompanying table with an oil lamp.

The dated feel of the room puzzled Ginger since

Beatrice Edgerton dressed in a completely modern fashion. Perhaps the house was too much for her, or the Edgerton finances weren't what they would like the world to think. Or it could just have been a matter of taste, or even compromise if the Edgertons had a version of Ambrosia in their family line hovering over matters.

Overnight, Mrs. Edgerton had gone from a ripe plum of a woman to a shrivelled prune. Her shoulders were slumped; her arms, hidden under a thin shawl, were pulled into herself; and her face had a crumpled appearance. Thurston Edgerton wasn't faring much better, and the redness in his face from the passion he'd once had for life had faded to grey.

Ginger felt dreadful about intruding like this. She shot a pleading look at Basil.

"Once again," Basil said, "I'm so sorry for your loss. We shall only take a moment of your time."

"Thank you," Mr. Edgerton said. "Please have a seat. I'll ring the bell for tea."

"Oh, please don't," Ginger said. She repeated Basil's claim. "We'll only be a moment."

"I'm very sorry to dredge this up, old chap," Basil said after he and Ginger had been seated. "But would you happen to know where Garrett went the night before the race?"

Thurston Edgerton shook his head. "He told me he

was going to go to bed early. He wanted to get some rest before the race. Why? What have you learned?"

After a brief pause and a glance at Ginger, Basil answered, "I'm afraid we've heard from the medical examiner. Do you know anything about secondary drowning?"

The Edgertons shared a look of confusion. Mr. Edgerton said, "No. Do tell, Basil, what is this about?"

"According to the medical examiner, secondary drowning is a situation that occurs after a near drowning experience," Basil explained. "The narrow vessels of the lungs are constricted and over time, fail to deliver oxygen to the brain."

"I don't understand," Mr. Edgerton said. "Garrett was a strong swimmer. He wouldn't have won a seat on the boat otherwise."

"He might've been overpowered," Ginger said softly.

Thurston Edgerton's passions returned. "Are you saying that my lad had his head held underwater by some hooligans!"

A whimper escaped Beatrice Edgerton's lips. "Why would anyone do that?"

Ginger answered, "That's what we're trying to find out."

"I know this is very upsetting," Basil added, "and I can assure you that we are investigating all angles. Is there anything you can think of, anything at all, that might be a clue to the identity of Garrett's attacker?"

"No," Beatrice said. "He was well liked by everyone."

Mr. Edgerton sighed and ran a hand through his hair. "I don't know if that's true, Beatrice."

"What do you mean?" asked Basil.

"I can't say for certain, but I heard him on the telephone talking to one of his chums, and he didn't sound too happy. More than once, too. When I asked Garrett, he just brushed me off, said it wasn't important."

"Do you happen to know who he was talking to?" Ginger said. "Did he mention any names?"

Mr. Edgerton shook his head with a weary sigh. "I didn't listen in, Mrs. Reed. I respected my son's privacy. Perhaps I shouldn't have."

Basil stood, and Ginger followed suit.

"We'll leave you in peace, my friends," Basil said. "But if you think of anything, anything at all that might help us with this case, please put in a call to the Yard."

Outside, Ginger let out a long breath. "That was frightfully unpleasant. Their pain was palpable. The whole matter is so disagreeable."

Basil lowered his chin in agreement. "The best we can do to help them is to find out what happened to their son."

CHAPTER NINE

*a*fter Basil had dropped Ginger off at her automobile, she returned to Feathers & Flair to retrieve Boss.

Felicia was there working as it were . . . if trying on new dresses from the latest delivery was work. Madame Roux simply rolled her eyes and shook her head. Despite several carefully formed "suggestions" from the shop manager, Felicia failed to get the hint.

"Think of it as an in-shop fashion show," Felicia said in her defence. "Customers want to see just how fabulous they might look in a new frock, how it fits on a live person."

"*Mon Dieu,*" Madame Roux muttered, then cheered as the bell rang announcing another customer.

Ginger thought Felicia was onto something, though, and made a note to pursue the idea of live modelling for her customers. She pushed through the heavy velvet curtain in search of Boss, but his bed was empty.

"Bossy? Where are you?"

Hearing the sound of his soft whine, she pushed aside some boxes. "Boss?"

The little dog scratched a small hole along the baseline of the wall.

"Oh dear," Ginger said. "Not mice?"

Boss barked and pawed at the hole. Ginger scooped him up. "Good boy, Boss. Mice in a dress shop shall never do."

Ginger gave Dorothy instructions to discreetly arrange for pest control to come in and repair the hole. Distaste crossed Dorothy's face, but she nodded politely. "Yes, madam."

"Mice could get into our fabrics and cause irreparable damage, not to mention the harm it could do to our reputation," Ginger said. Fabrics could be replaced, even the expensive imported kind Ginger ordered for her shop, but if word got out about a vermin infestation—oh mercy.

Keen to get out of the shop, Boss hopped into the Crossley with eager anticipation.

"Good news, Boss," Ginger said as she started the engine. "We're going to visit your friend Oliver."

Oliver Hill, a pet lover himself, had never had any

of his own. He was too busy looking after his parish-ioners, which Ginger knew first-hand, could be a lot of work. It was a short drive to St. George's Anglican Church, and a few minutes—and a few angry horn blasts—later, she drove down the cobbled drive and parked in a spot between the church and the parsonage.

Built in the eighteenth century, the limestone church had a square tower that opened to the narthex. A hall with a kitchen was attached to the nave, along with various other smaller rooms. Oliver and Matilda lived in the quaint little vicarage next door.

Ginger wanted to see her friends, but most of all she hoped to catch up with Bernard Ramsey, who was helping out with the jumble sale, an event to raise money for the needy of London.

Ginger, with Boss on her heels, walked into the bustle of activity in the hall and found Matilda sorting and folding.

"Matilda, love," Ginger said as they exchanged two quick cheek kisses. "How are you?"

"I'm fine." She placed a hand on her burgeoning belly. "I tire easily, which is to be expected."

"You must stay off your feet," Ginger said. She pulled a vacant wooden chair over. "I got Lizzie to put a bag of things together," she added. "I hope Clement dropped it off like he said he would."

"Yes, he did, and thank you. I always covet your offerings."

"I'm just happy they get used by those who need them."

"Are you here to see Oliver," Matilda said. "I think he's behind the rack over there near the back."

Ginger turned. She spotted Oliver but didn't see the man she'd come to find.

"I'm looking for Mr. Ramsey," Ginger explained. "I heard he might be working here as a volunteer."

"About that unfortunate death at the boat club, I imagine?" Matilda said. "Did you find out the cause? Did the poor lad have influenza?"

"I'm afraid it's worse than that." Ginger adjusted her hat. "Scotland Yard suspects foul play."

"No!" Matilda said.

"I'm afraid so. Please excuse me, my friend, I see Mr. Ramsey now and would like to have a word."

When Bernard Ramsey saw Ginger approach, Boss now snuggled in the crook of her arm, his eyes widened in interest.

"Good day, Mrs. Reed."

"Hello, Mr. Ramsey. I wondered if you could spare me a few minutes to discuss Garrett Edgerton's untimely death."

Mr. Ramsey's hands quivered slightly as he moved random objects on the table. "I didn't think you were here to shop or," he added with a snide tone, "*volunteer.*"

Ginger took issue at his inference that she was a social snob. "I'm not above doing my social duties, Mr. Ramsey."

"Fine. What do you want to know?"

"Were you and Garrett Edgerton friends?"

"We shared a pint on occasion, but I wouldn't consider him a chum. And in truth, not many blokes did."

"Why's that?"

"Garrett was the type of fellow who thought he was better than the others. He was going to be a titled Lord someday. He was more suited to those snooty universities like Oxford or Cambridge, but word has it that he couldn't pass the entrance exam." He swiped a hand over his oiled-back waves of hair. "Liked the ladies more than the books, if you know what I mean."

"Rather," Ginger said. "Where were you the night before he died?"

Mr. Ramsey narrowed his dark eyes. "That sounds like a question for the police, doesn't it? Why should I talk to you? Having a chief inspector for a husband doesn't mean you now have his authority, Mrs. Reed."

What a little upstart! Boss emitted a low growl. Even he didn't like Mr. Ramsey's attitude.

"That might be the case, Mr. Ramsey, however, I'm

sure the chief inspector will be interested in your response to my question, and when he asks it of you himself, he'll be far less charming. Wouldn't it be better for you to allow me to be your messenger? If you have nothing to hide, I would think it would be in your best interest to humour me."

"I was alone in my room, studying. Unlike Edgerton, I actually take my studies seriously."

"What are you studying, Mr. Ramsey?"

"I intend to become a chemist."

"A difficult course of study. I commend you." She wondered how Mr. Ramsey managed the laboratory work necessary when his hands tended to quiver.

"Not that I need your commendation, but thank you."

"Thank you for your time, Mr. Ramsey. I'm most certain we shall meet up again."

With Boss firmly in her grasp, Ginger pivoted on her heel. There was an absolute satisfaction that came with getting in the last word.

CHAPTER TEN

*P*ippins had seen Ginger arrive and waited to take her coat. It always amazed her. Even at his advanced age, he still managed to operate like he had eyes in the back of his head, and a spare ear to boot!

"Good evening, Mrs. Reed."

"Good evening, Pips. I'm afraid I've missed dinner."

"Should I ask Mrs. Beasley to prepare something?"

"That would be splendid, Pips."

Ginger found Felicia, now home from the shop, lounging on the settee in the sitting room and reading the latest Christie mystery. Boss disappeared through the door that led to the kitchen in search of his late supper as well.

Felicia looked up from her book. "You were busy

today," she said. "Must be nice to be able to drop into the shop and leave again at will."

"That is one of the advantages of owning one's shop," Ginger said unapologetically. She settled into her favourite chair, slipped off her pumps, and put her feet up on the ottoman.

"What were you doing, then?" Felicia said. She had no difficulties asking Ginger, or anyone else for that matter, questions that were none of her business.

"I have other work."

"Investigative work?" Felicia moved her creamy-white legs out from under her Elsa Schiaparelli designed day frock and leaned towards Ginger. "With Chief Inspector Husband, of course."

"We conducted a few interviews," Ginger admitted.

"What have you learned? Do you know what happened to poor Garrett?"

Ginger smiled at her eager young sister-in-law and responded teasingly, "Why? You can't use it in your novel, you know."

"I'm aware, but I can get ideas, can't I?" Felicia let her book drop closed. "Don't worry; I'll change the names to protect the innocent. Besides, I want to see that Garrett gets the justice he deserves."

Ginger considered her sister-in-law. "Actually, you may be able to help."

"How?"

"I know you don't partake in illicit drugs," Ginger started.

Felicia snorted. "Of course not. Why would you suggest such a thing?"

It was a thought that had nagged at the back of Ginger's mind after she'd left Mr. Ramsey. His tendency to fidget, the slight tremor in his hands. His interest in chemistry and pharmaceutical drugs. It could have been something as benign as a case of nerves. It probably was, but Ginger couldn't let the line of reasoning drop.

"I'm not suggesting that you take them," she said, "but I wonder if you're ever in with a crowd that does. At those clubs you like to sneak off to when Grandmother is sleeping."

Felicia shrugged a slight shoulder. "It happens."

"Have you ever seen members of the University of London rowing team partake?"

"That kind of thing happens behind closed doors," Felicia said. "It's only drinking and smoking that happen freely at the clubs. The oarsmen would be out on their ear if they ever used dope or were caught using it. But yes, I've seen many students at the clubs. I can't say I've seen any disappear into the back, but I haven't exactly been watching."

Lizzie tapped on the door and dipped in a short

curtsy. "Your tea has been delivered to your study, madam."

"Thank you, Lizzie," Ginger said. She called Boss, and he roused himself with a double hind-leg stretch in response. "Boss and I shall be at work in my study, Felicia, should you need us."

Felicia followed her out of the sitting room. "I'm going to the library to write. Inspiration has just struck! And don't think you've got out of telling me about those interviews."

Ginger's study had belonged to her father until his death. She had purposely retained the masculinity of style: dark wood panelling, large dark wooden desk, and an oversized burgundy leather chair. Smoke tunnelled up the flue of a grey stone fireplace, newly lit. She had never had the heart to remove George Hartigan's portrait, which hung humbly behind the door.

A tea tray with a pot of fresh tea, a dish of sliced lemons, and salmon sandwiches cut in quarters waited for her on the desk. Boss, who'd followed her in, sniffed then sat politely by Ginger's chair.

"Oh, Bossy, I do spoil you so," Ginger said as she chose one sandwich for herself and held another in her palm for her dog. Boss lapped it up gratefully then sauntered over to his bed by the fireplace.

Ginger smiled as she watched him sniff the

cushion then circle several times before settling in. "You certainly have the life, old boy."

She'd nicely finished eating and sipping most of a cup of tea when Pippins tapped on the door and entered.

"Mrs. Reed, there is a lady at the front door here for you."

"Oh?" Ginger raised a brow. She hadn't been expecting anyone. "Who is it?"

"A Mrs. Edgerton. She's quite determined to see you."

"Oh, really? Please ask her to wait in the drawing room. I'll be there in a moment."

Unlike the comfort of the sitting room, the drawing room was more formal and less used and somehow felt more appropriate for a meeting with a lady in such emotional pain.

In stark contrast to the Edgerton sitting room, Ginger's recent redecoration was open and airy. Even with the baby grand piano, which sat in the far corner, the room seemed neither cluttered nor overfull. The curtains, a lighter shade of rose, complemented the walls painted and papered with patterns of ivory and grey.

Dressed in all black, including a black veil that partially covered her face, Mrs. Edgerton sat upright in a new mint-green velour chair, her black-gloved hands folded primly on her lap. She made to stand when Ginger entered.

"Please remain seated, Mrs. Edgerton," Ginger said. She took the matching chair opposite. "How are you?"

Through tightly pursed lips, she said. "I'm angry, Mrs. Reed."

"Yes, that would be natural. Can I offer you some tea, perhaps?"

"No, thank you. I shan't be long."

"Very well. What can I do for you?"

"I'd like to hire you."

"Hire me?"

"You are Lady Gold of Lady Gold Investigations, are you not?"

"I am, but why do you need to hire me? You have London's finest working on your case."

"Yes, but they are all men. It's not that I don't have faith in your husband, Mrs. Reed, but, well, you've developed a bit of a reputation for solving crimes."

Ginger was pleased to hear it. "How nice of you to say, Mrs. Edgerton, but you must be aware that the chief inspector considers me a consultant. I've just come from attending his interviews."

"Perfect."

"I still don't understand why you want to hire me."

"You see, with the police, I fear they'll get

distracted once the next curious crime takes place, and I want someone who will stay focused on solving my son's murder."

"I see," Ginger said.

"And because I believe a charming lady such as yourself shall have a better chance getting those boys to tell the truth."

"Perhaps—"

"I don't want my husband to know I've come to you, Mrs. Reed, and I'd rather you didn't tell your husband I've been to see you either. I have my reasons for my discretion. I'll pay, of course."

Ginger didn't want to do anything that meant lying to Basil, even through omission.

"Mrs. Edgerton—"

"Do you have children, Mrs. Reed?"

"No."

"Then you might not be able to understand the devastation I feel right now. If only to appease a tiny bit of my grief, please say yes."

Mrs. Edgerton's plea stabbed Ginger in the heart, and despite her misgivings, she found herself agreeing to the arrangement.

"Splendid," Mrs. Edgerton said. She stood, then fished through her handbag and produced some pound notes. "A retainer."

Ginger took the money but was determined not to

bank it until the mystery behind Garrett's death was solved.

Mrs. Edgerton stood. "Thank you, Mrs. Reed. If you need to reach me, send a message through my maid, Hilda."

Pippins let Mrs. Edgerton out, and Ginger slumped into her chair, already regretting what she'd done.

$\mathcal{W}$henever she could, Ginger liked to take her horse, Goldmine, for a morning ride before she started her day. It often depended on the weather or the status of shipments due to arrive at the shop, or if a case she was consulting on had a lull.

Two out of three wasn't bad. Her case was new and anything but in a lull, but a ride would help her clear her head and think through the evidence they already had. Plus, it gave her time with Scout, a prospect that brought her joy.

After breakfast, she'd sent a message through Lizzie that she intended to ride and for Scout to have Goldmine ready to go.

"He's all ready for you, missus," he said. He smiled

his toothy smile. Pride shone through his blue eyes at having saddled and reined the horse on his own.

Ginger rubbed the gorgeous gelding on his golden nose. "Hello, handsome," she said. It wasn't a mere endearment. Goldmine was an Akhal-Teke originating from Turkmenistan. With their silky blond hair, these horses were considered one of the most spectacular breeds to gaze upon.

Ginger stared back at Scout and then at the Arabian. "What about Sir Blackwell." After they were married, Basil had moved his gelding, a generous wedding gift from his father, to her stables.

"Is Mr. Reed going wiv you?" Scout said. "Lizzie didn't say."

"Mr. Reed is busy with work today, I'm afraid," Ginger said. "But I thought you might like to join me."

"Really? I would!" Scout didn't waste a second in his effort to get Sir Blackwell ready. Ginger helped him with the heavy saddle but watched in admiration as Scout's rather spindly arms tugged on the straps under the horse's belly and tightened it with proficiency.

Once they were both in their saddles and ready to ride, Ginger took the lead out of the back lane. Kensington Gardens was close, and even though horses were plentiful on London streets, they were slowly getting outnumbered by automated vehicles. Ginger didn't like to take a chance with Goldmine and the possibility of a collision.

Cutting through Kensington Gore, they rambled past the exquisite Royal Albert Hall, a distinctively circular, and rather mesmerising concert hall. Ginger wondered at the fairytale-like romance between Prince Albert and Queen Victoria. Devastated by the prince's premature death, the Queen had been quite determined that her husband be remembered. Having lost one husband, Ginger couldn't bear to think about the possibility of such a thing happening again. She supposed that lightning didn't strike twice in the same place.

They trotted side by side, going east along the length of the Serpentine. Ginger had fond memories of the snake-like lake as Basil had proposed there.

"Are you happy with us, Scout?" Ginger asked. She'd caught the lad off guard, and the expression on his face tightened.

"Sure, I am, missus."

"You can be honest with me, you know."

"I know. I like it cuz I get enough to eat, and Mrs. Beasley's a good cook. I don't 'ave to worry about the cold anymore, though I shan't mind if Lizzie didn't make me have a bath quite so often."

Ginger laughed. "Actually, three times a week isn't a lot."

"But I miss my family. Marvin writes to me, once in a while. I try to write back to him, but my letterin's not so good. Lizzie helps me."

"How is Marvin?" Ginger couldn't imagine life in jail was all that great.

"He never talks about himself, just wants to know about me."

"He's your cousin. Of course, he cares about you."

"I miss my gang too."

"Your gang?"

"My mates. I don't have any at H-artigan H-ouse." Ginger suppressed a grin at Scout's exaggeration of the *h*'s. "Mr. Clement's fine," Scout continued, "but 'e's old like my uncle was. Lizzie's a girl and finks she's my muvver."

"Why do you say that?"

"Say what, missus?"

"That Lizzie thinks she's your mother?"

"I meant nothin' by it, missus. Just that she's always tellin' me to eat my vegetables, to sit up straight, and to fink about my future. 'What future is there for the likes of me?' I ask 'er. She says the good Lord's blessed me by pluckin' me off the streets and giving me a chance for learnin' and that I can be whatever I want to be if I play my cards right. Don't quite know what she means by that."

Ginger patted Goldmine on the neck as she

pondered Scout's words, shocked she felt as if they were burning her skin with a branding iron. Lizzie wasn't Scout's mother. If anyone should get that title, it should be Ginger. She was the one who had *plucked* Scout off the streets, after all.

She let out a long sigh. The truth was, Ginger hadn't been doing all the motherly things Lizzie had. Lizzie, having a lot of younger siblings to help out with, had had far more practice.

And Scout wasn't her child. He was her *ward*. He *worked* for her. He slept in the *attic*.

She sighed again.

Scout stared at her with a look of concern. "Is everythin' alright, missus?"

"Yes, it is. I'm glad you're happy with us. Perhaps there is something we can do about your lack of friends. A club to join, perhaps?"

"Oh, none of those types of clubs would accept the likes of me."

"Well, you can't go back to your gang, so what should we do about it?"

"I don't know, missus. Marvin would tell me to buck up and crack on." He smiled hard as if broadcasting his large new teeth would hold the sadness back.

Clement took a break from pruning the hedges

when he heard Ginger and Scout return from their ride.

"Good morning, Mrs. Reed," he said as he approached her. "Mr. Pippins gave me a message to give to you should I see you first. Mr. Reed rang from the Yard. He's requesting that you ring him back."

"Thank you, Clement," Ginger said as she dismounted. "Would you mind looking after Goldmine for me? Scout has Sir Blackwell to brush down."

Ginger hurried inside, curious as to what news Basil had for her. Using the telephone in her study, she dialled the Yard and asked to be put through to Basil's office.

"Basil, darling," she said once he was on the line. She was relieved when he'd answered. Her delay in responding could very well have meant waiting for who knew how long before he reached her again.

"Ginger, love, I'm heading back to the Imperial Institute, in search of Mr. Brooks and Mr. Pritchard. Would you care to join me in this consultation?"

"Of course. I've just got in from a ride, but I'll change quickly and meet you there."

"I've got work to catch up with here," Basil said. "Let's agree on one hour."

An hour was more than she thought she'd have, but still less than what she'd have liked.

"Very well. See you soon, love."

Grace, the part-time scullery maid, followed behind Ginger with a broom and dustpan in her hands. "I'm dreadfully sorry, Grace," Ginger said. "I didn't mean to drag in half the stable with my boots."

"It's your prerogative, Lady—, uh Mrs. Reed." Unlike Lizzie, Grace didn't live at Hartigan House and came in on whatever schedule Mrs. Beasley configured for her, and thus, had found it more difficult to remember Ginger's title change.

Before Ginger skipped up the staircase, she instructed, "Please let Lizzie know I'd like her to help me change."

Boss lifted his head in interest when she entered her room, whined a greeting, then promptly closed his eyes.

"What a lazy boy." Interfering with Boss' nap, Ginger scrubbed his ears. "How nice it must be to sleep all day long."

A soft tap on the door announced the arrival of Lizzie.

She bent at the knees slightly, then said, "Grace said you needed me, madam?"

"Yes. I'm to meet Mr. Reed in less than an hour, and I've just got in from a ride on Goldmine. I fear I smell of horse."

"I'll draw your bath, madam."

Ginger stripped out of her riding coat and breeches

and slipped into an Asian negligee before entering the hallway that led to the bathroom. Lizzie turned off the taps and handed Ginger a thick towel. "It's warm, madam. I added the lavender scent."

"Thank you, Lizzie. I wish I could soak for hours, but I'll be quick."

Lizzie left her alone, then Ginger removed her underthings and slid into the tub. The water was just the right temperature, and Ginger sighed with contentment. She let her mind go as she washed with soap, and reviewed her engagement with Mrs. Beatrice Edgerton.

Ginger supposed Mrs. Edgerton had a point about the police having too much on their plates to fully focus on catching her son's killer, but she knew that Basil wouldn't give up until he turned every last stone.

She wished she hadn't agreed to keep their agreement a secret. When Ginger had run an investigation before her nuptials, she hadn't felt obligated in any way to reveal everything to Basil, even after they were engaged.

Perhaps she wouldn't feel guilty now, except for the fact that Basil wasn't withholding anything from her. He'd even invited her to consult with him when they both knew gnarly Superintendent Morris wasn't thrilled at the prospect.

The problem with this case was that she had no

real suspects. No one with a firm motive. Inconsistent with Mrs. Edgerton's perception of her son, Garrett's team-mates didn't hold him in high regard. He crossed boundaries with ladies connected relationally to other men. Yet, none had given a clear example.

Lizzie turned her head to the side and held up the larger body towel. "Shall I lay out your outfit, madam?"

"That would be helpful. I'm attending meetings at the University of London so something suitable for that."

"Yes, madam."

By the time Ginger had dried off and returned to her room, Lizzie had laid out a two-piece, powder-blue Tailleur suit on the bed. Ginger smiled. Lizzie was worth her weight in gold.

CHAPTER TWELVE

That evening, around the family dinner table, Ambrosia was the first to remark on Basil's empty seat.

"Where's your husband?" she asked.

"He has to work late."

"Again?" Ambrosia said with a frown. "You're not having," she made an effort to lower her voice which wasn't effective at all, 'marital problems?'"

Stunned by Ambrosia's forthrightness, Ginger said, "No, Grandmother! Of course not."

"He probably can't stomach our family dinners," Felicia said, snidely.

"Nonsense." Ginger took a long sip of her wine. "This case is close to Basil, and he has to follow through on a few leads. Lord Edgerton is a personal friend. Naturally, Basil wants to do everything he possibly can to comfort him."

Felicia forced a yawn. "I'm extraordinarily tired. I think I'll go to bed early."

Ginger shot Felicia a look. Her "early to bed" nights often meant sneaking out until all hours.

"What on earth could've tired you out so?" Ambrosia said. "Scribbling books?"

"I'll have you know, Grandmama, that I worked hard all afternoon on my story." Felicia shook out her right hand. "My fingers ache from typing so much."

"Dear Lord, Felicia." Ambrosia exhaled sharply through her thin, wrinkled lips. "You need a new hobby. Why not take up embroidery or painting. Even French lessons would be an improvement."

"Oh, Grandmama. You're such an old goose." Felicia kissed her grandmother on the soft, loose skin of her cheek. "I'll see you at breakfast."

"I'm going to say good night as well," Ginger said.

"Don't tell me you've got a book to write too."

"No, but I do have a lot of bookwork to do. As I'm feeling rather tired, I'll take my ledgers up to my room and work until Basil gets in."

"Fine. I have Langley to keep me entertained. She's not a bad cribbage player."

"You could invite Mrs. Schofield round for a visit."

"Pfft. That old busybody?"

Ginger held in a grin. Ambrosia liked to fuss over decorum when it came to Mrs. Schofield, their widowed neighbour who was of similar age in body, but much more modern in her thinking.

"I suppose I should be charitable," Ambrosia said as Ginger suspected she would. Ambrosia was quite skilled at getting what she wanted under the guise of goodwill.

Ginger bypassed her study and went directly to the staircase that arched up to the upper floor. Once she got to Felicia's bedroom door, she stopped. She knocked, then entered before Felicia could beckon her inside.

Felicia had removed her day frock and sat at her dressing table wearing only her silk slip. Her makeup was on display, and she had one eye painted with a deep, smoky purple. An aqua-green evening gown, covered in sequins that shimmered under the electric light, lay across the four-poster bed.

"Did I miss a new trend in sleeping attire?" Ginger asked.

"You're frightfully funny, Ginger." Felicia continued with the second eye.

"I'm assuming you're going to a club."

"You'd be interested to know it's where the oarsmen like to spend their evenings."

"Felicia, you don't intend to do any sleuthing, do you?"

"I'm going to have fun, but if I happen to see or hear something of interest, I'm sure you won't mind."

"I do mind. It could be dangerous."

"I'm not exactly going to make an announcement."

"Fine. If you insist on going, I'm going with you."

Felicia paused, turned to face Ginger, and frowned. "You're a little old for this crowd."

"Please, don't soften the blow."

"But, with a little help from my friends," she motioned to the makeup sprawled on her table, "I could make you appear more youthful."

Ginger ducked to look at her image in the mirror. Compared to Felicia's porcelain skin, the fine lines around her own eyes and mouth seemed like canyons. "My hair is a problem as well," she said. "They've seen me up close."

"Don't you have a black wig? From one of your other cases?"

"I do. That might do the trick."

"Those boys have only seen you in a day dress. In one of those," Felicia's gaze flew to the dazzling dress on the bed, "and a different hair colour they'll never recognise you."

Ginger agreed. She had everything she needed in her room.

Unlike in America, clubs like the one Ginger and Felicia had entered weren't against the law, though certain activities sometimes associated with the clubs such as prostitution, gambling, and drugs were.

A five-piece jazz band's instruments blasted, and frolicking dancers filled the dance floor. There were fewer women than men, but enough to keep Ginger from feeling out of place. The barman was busy filling crystal glasses with amber liquid. A haze of cigarette smoke filled the room, filtering through dim lighting. It reminded her fondly of the speakeasies she and Haley had visited on occasion in Boston.

Felicia grabbed Ginger by the arm and shouted over the music. "There's an empty table near the back. It's the perfect spot to watch who goes in and out."

A waiter came by to take their order. Ginger ordered a gin and tonic for show. She didn't drink alcohol whilst on a case. She valued a clear head.

Felicia didn't seem to have the same reservation. She drank her cocktail in an alarmingly short amount of time.

"Ease up, Felicia," Ginger warned.

"Oh, boo on you. If I'd known you were going to be a wet rag, I wouldn't have agreed to let you come."

"Believe it or not, I don't need your permission."

"Oh, look," Felicia said, pointing towards the back of the room. "That bloke is from the rowing team, isn't he?"

Ginger grabbed Felicia's finger and pulled it down. She lifted her glass to conceal her face and looked at the lad. Indeed, she recognised him: Bernard Ramsey.

"If I could be a fly on the wall," Ginger said.

"Well, I can!" Felicia hopped to her feet. "Buzz, buzz, buzz!"

"No!" Ginger grabbed Felicia's arm. "What are you thinking?"

"I'm thinking I can go because no one cares who I am. I want to do this, Ginger. I fancied Garrett. It's the least I can do."

"If you don't come out in fifteen minutes, I'm coming after you."

"Fine. I'll just confirm if there's dope being taken, then I'll pretend to be ill. They won't like that."

"Fifteen minutes."

Felicia worked her charming smile on the man stationed at the back room door, and soon she was let in.

Ginger's heart dropped when she lost sight of Felicia. But what was she afraid of really? It wasn't like anyone would purposely hurt her. Why would they?

No, if Ginger was honest, she didn't trust her sister-in-law. Though Felicia denied it, she spent plenty of time gallivanting in places where drugs could be found. And even if she'd never tried drugs before, those young men could coerce her. Felicia had a good amount of alcohol in her system. She could be easily convinced. Letting her go alone had been a bad idea.

She had every intention of pushing herself past the man watching the door to extract Felicia when Felicia herself walked back into the room. She had an arm around her stomach and did indeed look ill. For the attendant's benefit, she said, "I think I've had too much to drink. Can you direct me to the loo?"

The man pointed, and Felicia headed straight there without giving herself away by looking at Ginger at all. Ginger chastised herself. How quick she was to think the worst of Felicia's character. She waited a moment, then followed her to the ladies.

"Felicia?"

She found Felicia checking all the cubicles and ensuring that they were alone. Felicia said, "They're definitely taking cocaine. Mr. Ramsey almost went to fists with another chap over who got to sniff the first row. It's quite disgusting when you think about it."

CHAPTER THIRTEEN

*T*he next day, Ginger accompanied Basil to the inquest.

"You're quiet today," Basil said as he pulled up to the Old Bailey courthouse. "Would it have something to do with the cigarette smoke I smelled on you last night? Or the black wig sticking out from under the bed?"

"Oh mercy," Ginger said. "You are a rather good detective, aren't you?"

She sighed. Even though she was investigating for Beatrice Edgerton and had promised not to tell Basil about her as a new client, she could share what she found with him. So long as the culprit was found.

"Felicia was bound and determined to go to one of her clubs last night, and I thought it might be prudent if I went along. She was certain members of the rowing team frequented the club, which made the disguise necessary because I've met many of them."

"What did you find out?"

"We only saw Mr. Ramsey enter the back room, and he was most definitely using cocaine." It saddened Ginger to have to mention the oarsman's name, knowing how Oliver and Matilda felt about him.

Basil scowled slightly. "How do you know for sure?"

Ginger explained Felicia's impulsive yet productive behaviour.

"She could've been in danger."

"I quite agree," Ginger said. "I didn't like it at all, but no harm came to her, and she did find out something that could be valuable to the case."

Basil inclined his head and stared at her from under the brim of his trilby. "And when, might I ask, were you going to relay your findings to me?"

"Well," Ginger said guiltily. "I couldn't very well tell you over breakfast with everyone listening. And I've told you now."

The inquest was held in a room not far from the courtroom. Amongst the attendees were the rest of the University of London rowing team sitting stiffly in a straight row rather like over-dressed fence posts; members of the sports faculty, including Mr. Jasper Ainsley, the coach, who hadn't brought his wife with him; and in the front seats, Mr. Edgerton and Mrs. Edgerton, who looked simply crushed.

Ginger and Basil took their seats. Basil removed his hat and set it on his lap. Ginger placed her handbag on the vacant chair beside her. She was saving the seat for Felicia who'd slept in and had promised to arrive by taxicab. Sergeant Scott came with Constable Braxton, prepared to give evidence along with Basil as law enforcers on the scene. Felicia arrived wearing a new, flowing rose and green spring design by Jeanne Lanvin. Heads turned when she breezed in. Even the oarsmen and a certain constable stopped what they were doing to look. By the smile on her made-up face and the flirtatious twinkle in her eye, Ginger knew that Felicia's delay had been intentional. Ginger held in a grin. Not so long ago, she would've done the same thing herself.

Felicia sat, provocatively crossed her legs, and gave the young men a show. "What have I missed?"

At that moment, the coroner entered the room.

"Nothing, darling," Ginger said. "It seems that you are right on time."

The coroner, an ageing man with more salt than pepper in his oiled-back hair, and a matching set of drooping jowls, called the room to order. He pushed a pair of round spectacles up the bridge of his nose and studied the papers in front of him. He cleared his throat.

"We're gathered here today to view evidence that may lead to the determination of the sudden and tragic cause of death of Mr. Garrett Edgerton."

A muffled sob emitted from Beatrice Edgerton that resounded through the high-ceilinged room.

"We share in the grief of these two parents whose son's life was cut short in the prime of his youth. It behoves us all to honestly and thoroughly give evidence to shed light on the nature of his death, and justice if a crime is indicated.

"It is such a shame for a sorrowful event to come on the heels of our exciting sporting event. Boat racing is a national institution, demonstrative of British character and instinct.

"I call upon Dr. Manu Gupta."

A soft shuffling of bodies filled the room as everyone turned and craned their necks, but the medical examiner appeared to be absent.

The coroner frowned. "It appears our medical expert has been delayed. Very well, we'll begin without him. I call upon Mr. Howard Pritchard."

Howard Pritchard entered the witness box. His eyes were red along with his nose, and he held a handkerchief at the ready. It appeared he was under the weather, and his usual air of confidence was sanded down on this occasion.

"Mr. Pritchard, you are the captain of the University of London rowing team, is that correct?"

"Yes, sir," Howard Pritchard said with a faint nasal tinge to his voice.

"And the deceased was a friend of yours?"

"He was friendly with all the oarsmen, sir."

"But not a particular friend with any?"

Mr. Pritchard hesitated. "I wouldn't say so."

The coroner stared back over the rims of his spectacles. "And why is that?"

"He was the reserve, sir. He exercised in his own time, so the rest of the team didn't spend much time with him."

"But he did race on that fateful day?"

Pritchard sniffed into his handkerchief. "Yes, sir."

"Why is that?"

"Er, there was a sudden vacancy."

"Explain?"

Mr. Pritchard's eyes searched out Mr. Ainsley before he spoke, obviously trying to choose his words carefully. "There was a breach of trust between Mr. Ainsley and Harry Brooks."

The coroner fingered one of the papers on the desk in front of him. "For the record, Mr. Brooks is the oarsman Mr. Edgerton replaced."

"Yes, sir."

"Do you know what Mr. Edgerton was doing the night before the race?"

"I do not."

"You weren't together?"

"No, sir."

"Do you have any idea how water got to be in the lungs of the deceased?"

"Definitely not.

"Thank you, Mr. Pritchard."

The coroner ran through the rest of the team who gave similar evidence. None were good friends with the deceased, none were with him the night before nor knew his whereabouts or pastimes. None knew anything about how Garrett could've drowned.

The coroner reviewed his papers, then said, "Would Miss Felicia Gold prepare to give evidence."

Felicia inhaled. She'd received a citation to attend, and being called wasn't unexpected, but Ginger knew from personal experience that it could be an over-whelming moment, nonetheless.

Felicia stood straight and walked down the aisle to the witness box like a Paris fashion model. Ginger couldn't have been prouder.

"Miss Gold," the coroner began. "It's my under-standing that when Mr. Edgerton collapsed to his death, you were conversing together at a party held at the team's boathouse. Is this correct?"

"Yes, sir, it is."

"Were you and Mr. Edgerton eating and drinking together?"

"Not eating, sir. We were drinking the champagne on offer."

"From the same source as everyone else?"

"Yes."

"Did Mr. Edgerton seem at all unwell at the time?"

"Well, he did tend to cough every so often," Felicia said. "His complexion appeared sallow to me, but I'd only just met him, so I didn't know if that was his usual appearance."

"You'd never met Mr. Edgerton before that afternoon?"

"No, sir."

"Very well, thank you, Miss Gold."

Ginger whispered in Basil's ear. "That was relatively pain-free."

The next up to give evidence was the Honourable Thurston Edgerton, and Ginger was most certain that his testimony would indeed be a rip in the already open wounds.

"We'll keep this as short as possible, Mr. Edgerton," the coroner said. "How did your son appear on the morning of the race?"

"He was excited. He'd always wanted to be an

oarsman on the long boat, and this was his opportunity to prove he belonged there."

"He didn't seem ill or under the weather in any way?"

"Well, he looked a little fatigued, but he'd been exercising a lot since getting the seventh seat. He only had a couple of days before the race."

"Is there any reason to believe that your son's death wasn't just a sad accident of nature? Is it possible that he simply lost his footing in the Thames and accidentally inhaled a bit of water?"

The muscles in Thurston Edgerton's face contorted as he worked to keep control of his emotions.

"I suppose it's possible, sir."

Dr. Gupta got to his feet. Ginger was amazed to see him, as she hadn't noticed him slipping in.

"Your Honour," he shouted. "I have new information."

"And you are?"

"Dr. Gupta, forensic pathologist."

"You've decided to join us, have you? Please come forward to give your evidence."

CHAPTER FOURTEEN

*D*r. Gupta had arrived late, so Ginger and Basil hadn't had a chance to speak to him that day. Ginger assumed the evidence he'd acquired had come in just that morning as Dr. Gupta was always prompt in ringing her with news.

"Proceed with your evidence, Dr. Gupta," the coroner said.

"New laboratory test results arrived this morning which determined the water components of the contents of the deceased's lungs weren't sourced from the Thames as one might've assumed, nor any natural reservoir, for that matter. It's tap water from London."

Ginger whispered to Basil. "That's interesting."

Basil nodded. "It'll make finding the scene of the assault somewhat easier to narrow down. At least, one would hope."

The judge called Basil next.

"Chief Inspector Reed," the coroner said, "it's my understanding that you were present at the after-race party hosted by Mr. and Mrs. Edgerton, and that you are a personal friend of the family."

"That's correct, sir."

"Please state your evidence from your position as criminal investigator."

"Of course.

"I was immediately on the scene when Mr. Garrett Edgerton collapsed and I checked for signs of life. The team doctor was in the house and confirmed what I had feared. Someone called the police, and Sergeant Scott and Constable Braxton arrived within twenty minutes and promptly took statements."

"What gave you reason to suspect foul play?" The coroner pointed to his paper. "It says here in my report from Scotland Yard that you're investigating."

"I couldn't conceive of a reason why a young man in his prime, in apparent good health and top athletic form, would die without warning."

"Go on."

"Then Dr. Gupta informed me of his autopsy findings. Mr. Edgerton died of a rare occurrence of secondary drowning."

"Yes, I've been informed." The coroner's chin fell as he read from his report. "Water trapped in the lower part of the lungs constricting oxygen flow to the brain." He returned his focus to Basil. "Any reason not to assume water emergence was a mere accident?"

"Garrett Edgerton was an expert swimmer as are all the team members."

"But now we know that he didn't submerge himself in the river. Perhaps he lost his footing in the bathtub?"

"According to the postmortem report," Basil said, "there were no abrasions to Mr. Edgerton's skull, something that would provide a reason for him to become unconscious for the length of time it would take to inhale the water."

"What is it, exactly, you are suggesting, Chief Inspector?"

"It's my theory that Mr. Edgerton was held forcibly underwater. Long enough for him to struggle and inhale but not long enough to lose his life at that moment."

"As you said, Chief Inspector, Mr. Edgerton was in top athletic form. Surely he would've resisted?"

"There were bruises on his wrists, sir. Somebody held him in a tight grip."

"If that were the case, why did he not report it?"

"That is precisely what I'm investigating, sir."

"I see. And do you have suspects in mind? Motives?"

"The investigation is ongoing."

"I'll need a little more than that, Chief Inspector, if I'm going to give you the charge you desire."

Basil's gaze moved to Ginger, and she nodded a subtle encouragement. They were in the middle of the mire now.

"At the moment I'm investigating three persons of interest, sir. Mr. Brooks, Mr. Ainsley, and Mr. Ramsey."

A wave of gasps and murmurs filled the room with three rather bold protestations from the named men.

"Order!" the coroner demanded. To Basil, he asked, "And motives?"

"In the case of Mr. Brooks, anger at Mr. Edgerton taking his place; with Mr. Ainsley, jealousy arising from a suspected liaison between his wife and the deceased; and with Mr. Ramsey, possible dope dealing."

After a moment of stunned silence an uproar erupted.

"Enough! Enough, I say," the coroner shouted. "Do be quiet, or I'll have you all charged with contempt."

The coroner shuffled his papers. "As you know, this is not a trial but an inquest. As a result of the evidence given today, I'm declaring Mr. Garrett Edgerton's death manslaughter by a person or persons yet unknown."

CHAPTER FIFTEEN

"Well, that was jolly well awful," Felicia said.

Ginger couldn't have agreed more. Basil had left them to see to Thurston and Beatrice, helping them outside to their automobile. Ginger hoped Mr. Edgerton had had the foresight to keep his driver waiting.

Dr. Gupta joined them with an apologetic look on his face. "I'm so sorry to have sprung the results of the lab reports on you like that, but I'd only just received them myself. I fear your husband hadn't come prepared to be interviewed by the coroner in such a manner."

"Garrett must've known who attacked him," Felicia said. "It's a wonder he never told anyone."

"Perhaps he had his reasons," Ginger said. "Shame, humiliation. Guilt?"

Dr. Gupta tipped his hat. "I'll leave the sleuthing to you two fine ladies. Please give the chief inspector my regards."

Felicia's attention was now focused elsewhere, and Ginger looked in that direction to see. Constable Braxton had once again caught her eye.

"If you will excuse me, Ginger, I'm going to say hello to Constable Braxton and thank him for his help in solving this case."

"Haven't you already thanked him," Ginger said. "And he hasn't solved this case."

Felicia smirked. "Either way, I'm bound to do my duty as a thankful citizen. I'll find my own way home."

"Don't you have to work today?" Ginger said.

"Oh, yes. I'll find my way to the shop."

Ginger watched as Felicia sashayed across the room, the hem of her silvery-grey crepe de Chine frock caressing her calves, and hoped her sister-in-law would keep within the bounds of propriety. If not for her own sake, then for poor Ambrosia's!

Basil returned with a deep frown etched on his face. Even when serious, his brooding hazel eyes captivated Ginger. She linked her arm with his. "Are they all right?"

"I wouldn't say so. I'm afraid they have a long road

ahead before either of the Edgertons smile with sincerity again."

"It's so sad."

They walked outside to Basil's Austin, and he opened the passenger door for her. She slipped inside and checked her lipstick and hair in the rearview mirror. When she'd finished, Basil readjusted it for his use without complaint, a sure sign he loved her.

"What's next?" Ginger asked.

"We need to find the person guilty of the crime that led to Garrett's death."

"Obviously, but do you have a plan? What's your next step, Chief Inspector?"

With a half grin, he threw the question back at her. "What would you do, Lady Gold?"

"Determine who had a motive. Who had a reason to get into a heated argument?"

"Sounds like a rather lengthy discussion," Basil said. "Shall we make a list over luncheon?"

There was a cosy French bistro nearby, warmly decorated in tones of yellow and red, which Ginger frequented, and thankfully, a round table with two matching wrought iron chairs was available. Ginger ordered their famed French onion soup, whilst Basil stayed with the more traditional English meal of steak and kidney pie.

As they waited for their orders to arrive, Ginger

asked, "Might I have your notepad, love? And your pencil? I find it helps me to see things once they're written down."

Basil removed his notepad and pencil from his jacket pocket and handed her both items. She opened the notepad to a blank page.

Ginger created two columns. "Names and motives. Who's first?"

"Harry Brooks," Basil said. "Over seat seven."

Ginger scribbled the name and motive, then said, "Garrett didn't actually take it from him. The coach was responsible for that." She spoke as she jotted down the next suspect. "Jasper Ainsley, jealousy."

"If he was jealous about Brooks, why would he assault Garrett?"

"He found out that Garrett was also enjoying the company of his wife, but it was too late for Mr. Ainsley to replace Garrett as well."

Basil grinned. "Good motive, Lady Gold."

"Thank you, Chief Inspector," Ginger replied playfully. "Next?"

"Bernard Ramsey. Perhaps Garrett discovered Ramsey's fondness for illicit drugs and threatened to report him."

"He'd have lost his spot on the team," Ginger said as she jotted the notes down. "Perhaps even been expelled. Excellent motive."

Basil elaborated. "He might've been under the influence of drugs, got into a scuffle with Garret, and managed to get the upper hand. I've seen the effects of cocaine on men in France. As you know, it was widely used by the troops before the government realised how addictive it was."

"What about Howard Pritchard?" Ginger asked. "Mr. Pritchard downplays his childhood friendship, but perhaps it was deeper than that. Perhaps Garrett betrayed a loyalty in some way?"

"Holding a bloke's head underwater could be a crime of passion," Basil said. "It's among our weaker motives."

Ginger agreed, then added, "That leaves Miles Brassey, Jude Fellows, John McMillan, and Jerry McMillan."

"Those fellows have weak or no motive at all," Basil said.

Ginger glanced at Basil regretfully. "I hate to do this, love, but I must." She wrote down Thurston Edgerton's name.

"No," Basil said. "That's nonsense."

"You're too close to it," Ginger said. "Take a step back and look at it through your eyes as a detective and not as a friend. When you accompanied the Edgertons to their vehicle after the inquest, did either of them have anything to add?"

"No. I do know that Thurston and Garrett had a difficult relationship, and they didn't see much of each other as a rule."

"Did they argue?" Ginger asked with caution.

"Not more than most parents do with their children."

"Has anyone asked Thurston what he was doing the night before the race? What if Garret upset his father to the point where Thurston lost his control and wanted to teach his son a lesson?"

Looking disgruntled, Basil picked up the notepad and flipped through until he found the page he wanted. He quoted, "Stayed in that night with Beatrice, finalising details for the party at the boat club."

"So, they're each other's alibi," Ginger said. Basil narrowed his gaze in disapproval but relented. "It's a motive worth investigating.

"I'll call in later to confirm what they said."

"I'm sure they were," Ginger said. "Like the police often say, it's a matter of form."

Basil grunted, but his eyes flashed with a look of esteem for Ginger. She smiled back but jumped her gaze to a plant before her detective husband could see she was keeping something from him. She hoped she was wrong about Thurston, for Beatrice's sake.

Their meals arrived, and they spoke of other

things. Perhaps they should go and watch a play in the West End or a performance at the opera house?

They talked about music and American films. Ginger loved how she and Basil enjoyed more than just murder in common, though, all the while, Ginger couldn't forget about the names she'd written down: Harry Brooks, Mr. Ainsley, Bernard Ramsey, Howard Pritchard, and Thurston Edgerton.

CHAPTER SIXTEEN

The next logical step was to begin second interviews with the subjects on their new list, and once they'd finished their meal, Basil drove them to the Imperial Institute.

The senior tutor assisted them in their quest to track down Mr. Harry Brooks, and they found the former oarsman in the courtyard, legs crossed as he sat on one of the benches with a book on his lap.

Basil thought the young man resembled Garrett in size and looks, though where Garrett had had a playful countenance, Harry Brooks scowled as if he had a thundercloud over his head.

He spoke first. "What do you want with me? I wasn't even at the race."

"Mr. Brooks," Basil said, "let us start with a proper

introduction. I'm Chief Inspector Reed, and this is my consultant, Lady Gold."

Harry Brooks' gaze lingered on Ginger with mild interest before turning back to Basil. "Like I said, I wasn't there."

"Can you recall where you were the night before the race, Mr. Brooks?" Ginger asked.

Harry Brooks shrugged a muscular shoulder. "I'm afraid I can't. Off drinking in some pub, likely, washing my blues away."

"Why were you removed from the team?" Basil asked.

"Don't you read the rags? The scandal surpassed the reach of the university paper to the *London Daily Herald*. Mrs. Ainsley and I had an attraction, you could say," Mr. Brooks said bitterly. "In my defence, she was the one to pursue me, yet ultimately, I was the one punished for it."

"Are you saying you were powerless to resist her charms, Mr. Brooks?" Ginger asked.

Harry Brooks scoffed. "Have you met Carol Ainsley?"

"A little self-control goes a long way," Basil admonished.

"I daresay. Am I here for a sermon?"

"You didn't like Garrett Edgerton, did you?" Basil said.

"I had nothing against him personally."

"But he took your place on the team?" Ginger said. "Your place of glory."

"If not him, then it would've been someone else. What's this all about anyway? The chap died in full view of dozens of people without anyone laying a hand on him."

"The coroner's report indicated that Mr. Edgerton died as a result of foul play," Basil said.

"I know, I was there," Mr. Brooks said without empathy. "Well, it certainly had nothing to do with me. Like I said, I was in the pubs. I can get you names of people who saw me there."

"That would be splendid," Basil said. "I'll get an officer from the Yard to contact you."

As BASIL and Ginger walked back to his motorcar, Basil felt the knot that had been growing in his chest tighten. "That was spectacularly unhelpful."

"You never know what nugget might be mined from this conversation at a later date." Basil loved how his wife always looked at the world through rose-coloured glasses. He could learn a thing or two from her.

"Have you spoken to the coach, yet?" Ginger asked.

Basil shook his head. "That's next on my list, along with Mr. Pritchard if he's out of the doctors yet."

Another enquiry to the senior tutor revealed that Mr. Ainsley had gone, "the boat club more than likely," and that Howard Pritchard was laid up in his room recovering from "a nasty cold or something." The tutor gave Basil directions, and he and Ginger walked around the courtyard in search of Mr. Pritchard. After a false turn or two, Basil and Ginger finally happened upon Mr. Pritchard's room. He responded to Basil's knock by calling out. "I'm too ill to get the door. Come in at your own risk."

Basil glanced at Ginger, with a look that said she was free to stay outdoors.

"I think not, Chief Inspector," she said, her pretty little chin tilting up defiantly.

"Very well. We shall risk together and perhaps die together," Basil said.

"Oh, that's quite morbid, love."

Mr. Pritchard reclined on his bed, fully clothed, thankfully. He appeared long, with pointy sock-covered feet reaching the edge of the much shorter bed. He made no move to greet them.

"You lot are a revelation," he said, sounding nasal.

"You were expecting someone else?" Basil asked.

"I wasn't expecting anyone." He pointed at his

swollen nose. "No one wants to hang around this red nozzle. What do you want, anyway?"

"We'd like to ask a few questions about Garrett Edgerton."

"Oh, yes. His troubles make my current bout of suffering seem insignificant. I can't believe he just dropped dead like that. Poor bloke."

"How well did you know Mr. Edgerton?" Ginger asked.

"It depends on what you mean by the question," Pritchard said vaguely. "I've known him since childhood. We were at junior school together. I suppose you could say we were chums back then."

"But not now?" Basil asked.

"Let's just say Edgerton, and I didn't see eye to eye on a lot of matters."

Basil prompted. "Such as?"

"The usual. Girls, money, what it means to be here at this uni."

"Can you elaborate?" Ginger asked. She tucked the red lock of hair that pressed against her chin behind her ear and flashed the smile that still made Basil grow weak at the knees.

Pritchard's eyes locked with Ginger's, and Basil had to resist hitting him around the head.

"Not to be insensitive, Mrs. Reed, but Edgerton

had a 'love them and leave them' philosophy when it came to the ladies."

"I suppose that might've made some of them angry?" Ginger said.

"Quite right. If Edgerton had got a pound every time a gal slapped his face, he could have bought his own boat."

"Do you have names?" Basil said.

Pritchard shook his head. "Edgerton might've been a cad, but he didn't kiss and tell."

"What did you mean about his attitude toward this uni?" Ginger asked.

"He didn't care if he was here or not. He's got an elitist attitude, sorry, had an elitist attitude. Better suited for the posh hallways of Oxford or Cambridge, but he didn't have the will to do anything with his life. Many of us are here because we don't have a trust fund to pay our way for the rest of our lives."

So that was his money issues, Basil thought.

"Where were you the night before the race, Mr. Pritchard?" Basil asked.

Pritchard had a hanky to his nose, but his eyes relayed his unease at the question. "I don't know. Who remembers stuff like that? My head's stuffed. I can barely remember rising this morning."

"Try harder," Basil pushed.

Pritchard let out a martyr's sigh. "The night before

the race, yes, I was studying. Big exams coming up, you see."

"In the library or a study room?" Ginger asked.

"In my room," Pritchard huffed. "What is this anyway? Why does it sound like I need an alibi?"

"As you know, the coroner ruled Mr. Edgerton's death foul play, Mr. Pritchard," Basil said. "Can you think of any reason that someone would want to hurt Mr. Edgerton?"

Pritchard rolled his eyes. "Haven't I already made a case for that? He was an insensitive cad who, I might add, stole Brooks' seat in the race."

"Do you have a girlfriend?" Ginger asked.

Pritchard smiled crookedly. "I don't take up with married ladies, Mrs. Reed." He raised a hand before Basil could protest. "But that's just me. Edgerton didn't have such qualms."

"I thought he didn't kiss and tell?" Basil said.

"Sometimes, rumours fly."

"Did Mr. Edgerton ever have a liaison with Carol Ainsley?" Ginger asked.

Pritchard snorted. "I see why you bring the missus along, Chief Inspector. She's good."

CHAPTER SEVENTEEN

*J*asper Ainsley had just finished an afternoon row on the Thames in what looked to Ginger to be a single-person scull. She confirmed this with Basil, who'd spent some time before the race teaching her the different types of boats. "Sculls—where each person uses two oars, one per hand. And sweeps, where both hands manage a single oar."

"That's right," Basil said as he glanced toward the coach. "I wonder if that's the boat Garrett trained in."

Basil hurried towards the coach to offer his assistance.

"Out for a row?" Basil said, stating the obvious.

"Yes. Gets my blood going. Helps me to relax, especially after the circus that inquest proved to be."

Ginger stood to the side as the men carried the

scull into the ground level of the boathouse and raised it amongst the other longer boats. Mr. Ainsley returned the oars to the brackets on the wall where they were stored.

"Did you the two of you want to go for a row?" the coach asked, then took in Ginger's dress suit. "I hope you came with a change of clothes."

"Not today," Basil said, "but perhaps we can take you up on your offer sometime." He glanced at Ginger with a grin. "You'd like to go rowing with me, love, wouldn't you?"

"Of course." Her response was genuine. She'd never been rowing, but Ginger was always up to trying something new.

"Then what are you here for?" the coach asked.

"We have a few questions regarding Garrett Edgerton."

Jasper Ainsley's brow crumpled into thin lines.

"You don't mind if we chat over a pot of tea, do you?" Ainsley asked.

"That would be wonderful," Ginger said.

They headed up the wooden steps that led to the back door of the club which opened into the kitchen area. Mr. Ainsley put the kettle on and scooped loose tea leaves into the teapot.

"I'm going to change out of these wet wooly trousers if you don't mind," the coach said.

"Not at all," Basil said. "Is it all right if we look around a bit?"

"Suit yourselves."

The open room where the festivities had taken place after the race looked larger and echoed even louder when vacant. Ginger remembered the party and the people who'd been eating tiny sandwiches and drinking champagne as they mingled. She and Basil walked to the spot where Garrett had fallen to his death. Someone had mopped the wooden floor since then, and a strong lemon scent lingered.

Ginger opened the unlocked glass door that led to the veranda, and leaned on the railing in the precise spot Felicia and Garrett had been standing when they watched the revellers along the riverside.

"It's always odd to return to the scene of the crime," Basil said. "Though technically, the crime didn't happen here, just the consequences of it."

The kettle whistle blew and echoed through the hall. Ginger and Basil returned to the kitchen just as Mr. Ainsley finished pouring the boiling water into the pot. He retrieved three cups and saucers from one of the cabinets and provided sugar and milk, the latter from the cold cupboard, along with the necessary teaspoons.

Once they each had their tea poured and had added sugar to their taste, they sat at a round table. The coach repeated the question he'd posed earlier. "What are you here for? I know Edgerton breathed his last breath here, but what does that have to do with me?"

"The coroner mentioned secondary drowning," Basil said. "Do you know what that is?"

The coach sipped his tea then lowered his cup. "Enlighten me."

Basil explained the science as Dr. Gupta had related it. "It occurs after a traumatic water event such as a near drowning."

"All my oarsmen are excellent swimmers. It's a requirement of the sport."

"Someone held Garrett's head underwater," Ginger said, "the night before the race."

"So the coroner said. Still, I don't understand why the experience caused his death. He was a strong, virile youth."

How virile? Ginger wondered. To the extent that Garrett would have a liaison with the coach's wife right under the coach's nose?

Mr. Ainsley continued, "Surely he could've coughed up whatever water lingered in such a situation."

"Mr. Edgerton had a severe case of bronchial pneumonia as a child which resulted in scarring in the finer parts of his lungs," Basil explained. "Had he gone to the doctor, or perhaps hadn't exerted himself with something as physically demanding as a rowing race, he would've recovered."

"I'm sorry to hear that."

Basil looked at Ginger in a way that warned her he was about to dive into treacherous territory.

"Mr. Ainsley, it's come to our attention that your wife was quite, er, pally, with some of the athletes."

The coach's eyes narrowed and glazed with anger. With tight lips, he said, "You can't believe everything you hear, Chief Inspector."

"Why did you remove Mr. Brooks from the team?" Ginger asked. "Was it not because he'd become involved with your wife?"

Mr. Ainsley slapped the table, and all three cups of tea spilled a portion of their contents.

"What happens between my wife and me is my business, Mrs. Reed." He stood, staring Basil down. "It would behove you to rein in your own wife, Chief Inspector. I'll let you find your way out."

With that, the coach disappeared out of the door.

Ginger sipped her tea, then said, "Well, that went well."

"Indeed. I'd say our dear coach has a problem keeping his temper in check."

"He's certainly strong enough to hold a fellow down against his will."

"He learned about Brooks and sacked him," Basil

said, "then hearing the replacement was also involved with his wife, became physical."

"If only Garrett had reported this alleged abuse," Ginger said.

"Then he'd have had to admit to his illicit affair. I think Edgerton would've seized his son's allowance had the truth come out."

"It appears our Garrett was a wild one," Ginger said, regretfully. She wished she hadn't agreed to work for Beatrice Edgerton. Now she was ethically bound to tell her everything she was learning about her pampered son, and Ginger didn't relish the thought one bit.

CHAPTER EIGHTEEN

Ginger asked Basil to drop her off on Regent Street so she could oversee a new shipment of exotic fabrics from India due to arrive that afternoon. Madame Roux greeted her at the door with an excited gleam in her eyes.

"They've arrived, Mrs. Reed. I'm afraid we couldn't resist having a quick look. They are oh, so, *si beaux!*"

Ginger hurried across the marble floor and pushed through the velvet curtains to find Felicia, Dorothy, and Emma examining the rolls.

"Ginger," Felicia said. "I simply must have a gown made from this silk georgette. And a turban." She turned to Emma. "You could make that for me, couldn't you?"

"Yes, Miss Gold," Emma said cautiously. "If Mrs. Reed approves."

Ginger chuckled. "I'm sure we can work something out, providing you agree to give Emma a bonus, Felicia."

"I'll work extra shifts if necessary, but I can't imagine my wardrobe without it."

Dorothy looked a little forlorn, and Ginger made a note to talk to Felicia about restraining herself in front of those who couldn't simply make a request for the finest original frock and have it happen.

The shop bell rang announcing a potential customer. Ginger said to Felicia, "You can start by attending to whoever it is that's just walked in."

"Straightaway, Mrs. Reed," Felicia said, then left the back room with a sense of purpose.

To Dorothy, Ginger asked, "How are things going on the second floor?"

On the second floor, factory items hung on racks with identical frocks available in several sizes. The trend for good-quality factory-made dresses was on the rise, especially with the younger crowd who wanted the things they wished for quickly.

A sense of guilt weighed heavily in Ginger's heart when she saw Boss' empty bed. She hated leaving her dog at home without her for such long stretches. She was thankful that Scout and Lizzie looked after him whilst she was out, but Boss was not only her responsibility but her last breathing tie to her father who'd given him to her as a gift after Daniel had died.

Ginger went back into the front of the shop, pleased to see both Felicia and Madame Roux busy with return customers, and picked up the heavy, ornate receiver of the shop's telephone. She dialled Hartigan House and relayed a message through Pippins for Clement to drive Boss to her. It was an indulgence, Ginger admitted, but Clement was in her employ to perform driving duties.

In the back, Ginger and Emma sorted through fabrics and discussed designs. The time flew by, and before she knew it, Clement had arrived with Boss. Felicia intercepted him at the front door and carried the small dog to the back before the eyebrows of their patrons could be raised.

"Boss, you spoiled thing," Felicia said as she handed him to Ginger. "Clement wants to know if you'd like him to leave the Crossley behind. He's offered to take a bus back to Hartigan House."

"How thoughtful of him," Ginger said. "It would be convenient to have my motorcar at hand. But tell him to take a taxicab." Ginger placed Boss on his bed, then retrieved her black Coco Chanel handbag.

Unsnapping the reflective, interconnecting C-clasps that Miss Chanel had made her trademark, she removed a few coins and handed them to Felicia. "Give him this to cover his fare."

It became apparent that Boss wasn't a bit sleepy. He greeted Emma with a wet nose, and she scrubbed his ears. "I love it when Boss comes to visit. He brings so much joy to a room."

Ginger couldn't have agreed more. Boss sniffed about the back room, which caused Ginger to worry that their rodent problem hadn't been solved, but after a few minutes of intense sniffing, Boss appeared satisfied. He returned to his bed, circled it several times, collapsed with his chin propped on one of his paws, and closed his eyes. Immediately, a soft snore emitted from his small body.

Emma laughed. "I wish I could fall asleep so quickly."

"Have you tried circling your bed first?" Ginger said with a smile.

"I haven't. I'll make a point to do so tonight."

Ginger was behind the cash counter in the shop when the postman arrived with the afternoon post. Felicia rushed over.

"Anything for me?" she asked.

Ginger raised a brow. "Why would you have letters

delivered to Feathers & Flair?" Before Felicia could answer her, Ginger spotted an envelope addressed to Miss Felicia Gold. "A publisher?"

Felicia snatched the letter from Ginger's hand. Lowering her voice, she explained, "I didn't want Grandmama to intercept it. I thought it best to give them this address."

"Are you going to open it?" Ginger asked.

Felicia had the envelope pressed tightly against her chest. "I'm afraid."

"Perhaps we should go into Madame Roux's office for a little privacy."

Madame Roux's office was a small room off the back area, not much larger than a cupboard. Ginger and Felicia squeezed inside with Ginger turning on the electric light and closing the door behind them.

"You can open it now, love."

"But what if he hates me."

"He can't hate *you*. He doesn't know who you are." Ginger offered Felicia the letter opener from Madame Roux's desk.

Taking a deep breath, Felicia sliced the letter open, removed the folded sheet of paper, opened it, and read.

Her countenance collapsed. "It's a rejection. I'm a terrible writer. I should just give up!"

"Oh, love," Ginger said, pulling Felicia into a sisterly embrace. "You mustn't give up. There are other publishers." As to Felicia's claim about being a terrible writer, Ginger could give no opinion—Felicia had refused to let Ginger read her manuscript.

"No, Grandmama is right. I'm wasting my time."

Ginger clasped Felicia's shoulder. "That is simply not true. If it's in your heart to write, then you should do it. Publishers are dolts. You've heard of Kenneth Grahame, and the American F. Scott Fitzgerald. They, like many others, were rejected by publishers before becoming a success. I beseech you not to give up."

Felicia sniffed into her handkerchief. "Oh, Ginger. You're a peach. I don't know what I'd do without you."

"I'm quite fond of you as well," Ginger said jovially.

A knock on the door interrupted them. "There's a telephone call for you, Mrs. Reed. It's your butler on the line," Dorothy said.

Ginger gave Felicia another quick hug before leaving her alone to answer the phone.

"Hello, Pippins. Is everything all right?" She braced herself. Pippins wouldn't call her at the shop if the situation didn't merit her immediate attention. Had the pipes in the kitchen burst again? Were uninvited guests now sitting in the drawing room, awaiting her arrival home?

"It's young Scout, madam. We've searched the garden and the house, but we can't find the lad."

"How long's he been gone?" It wouldn't be that unusual for a boy Scout's age to wander about the streets once in a while.

"Since yesterday, madam."

Oh mercy. *Yesterday?*

CHAPTER NINETEEN

*a*fter dropping Ginger off at her shop, Basil did his best to track Bernard Ramsey down, finally catching up with him at the Crown and Sceptre, a pub his senior tutor had said was a favourite of the oarsman.

Feeling the need for an energising jaunt, Basil opted for the ten-minute walk. The pub, only steps from the busy streets, was tucked away behind a neglected hedge, which created a sense of seclusion. A cobbled path of cracked stones led to a heavy wooden door that Basil thought might be an original from the seventeenth century. He had to put his weight into the motion to push the door open.

Dimly lit with oil lamps, the interior had low ceilings, rough, exposed timbers, and scarred wooden tables and chairs. Basil spotted Ramsey sitting alone next to an opaque window, dulled by years of grime. Basil guessed this pub was owned and operated by men, and a cursory glance proved that not one female had dared to enter. Basil's lips twitched. Ginger would've loved to make an entrance here, and he regretted that she wasn't with him for this interview.

Bernard Ramsey, though athletic and a power-house, was the nervous type. His knees jumped under the table, and he tapped his fingers along his well-formed arms. When Basil unceremoniously claimed the empty chair across from him, Ramsey jerked

"What? Hello?" Ramsey said in response.

"Good afternoon, Mr. Ramsey." Basil removed his hat. "You don't mind if I join you?"

"Not that I could say no," Ramsey said, "but there are other empty seats if you bother to look around. I'm not really up to company."

"I've been looking for you. You're a little hard to pin down."

Ramsey took a large drink of ale and wiped the foam from his lips with the back of his arm. "I'm sure it was a simple thing for you, Chief Inspector. It's what they pay you for, isn't it? Detecting?"

"Indeed. I have a few questions regarding Garrett Edgerton."

"I gave my evidence at the inquest. I have nothing more to add."

"To your knowledge, did Garrett ever use cocaine?"

Ramsey blinked hard. "That's illegal. No one at the uni would risk it."

"Not even you?"

Ramsey shook his head slowly. "Nope."

Basil pointed at his greying temples. "You know what I think, Ramsey? I think you and Garrett did enjoy a sniff or two, and the night before the race, you argued. Your disagreement got physical, and somehow you outmanoeuvred Edgerton, got the advantage, and dunked his head in some water. The toilet?" It was a bluff to see how Ramsey responded to the charge. Basil was rewarded.

"Stuff and nonsense! You can't prove anything."

"I can't prove who assaulted Edgerton, not yet, but I shall. I can confirm that you are acquainted with cocaine because I have a witness. You were seen by a reliable witness in the back room of a club."

Ramsey's ruddy cheeks drained of colour. His knees jiggled under the table, and he attempted to hide his face behind his pint of ale. "I don't know what this Miss Gold saw, but it wasn't me."

"She's a credible witness, Mr. Ramsey," Basil said.

"Her word against mine, I'd say. Besides, she was a little lit up herself to know for sure what she saw."

Basil paused to give Ramsey a chance to realise his

slip. Then he said. "So you admit to seeing her, then? To being in the back room."

Ramsey stiffened, his focus darting about like a frightened animal. "I-I-I'm not saying another word without my solicitor present."

"That sounds like an admission of guilt," Basil said, pushing.

"It's an admission that I'm not guilty, Chief Inspector, at least not of manslaughter like the coroner said."

"Not manslaughter." Basil leaned in. "Murder."

CHAPTER TWENTY

Ginger was frightfully thankful that Clement had left her Crossley for her. She explained her urgency to Madame Roux, scooped up Boss and her handbag, and headed out of the door.

"Wait for me," Felicia said, running along the marble floors whilst holding on to her hat.

Ginger drove the Crossley as fast as she could through narrow streets. The right tyre hit the kerb—the chassis lifted and dropped back to the concrete with a thump. Boss whined as he hit the floor.

"So sorry about that, Bossy," Ginger said. The worry in her chest grew as each minute passed.

"We're not going to help Scout if you crash trying to get there," Felicia said from the back seat. "He's probably been found already. You know how he can play up sometimes, the little rascal," she added. "He's just trying to get your attention. You *have* been rather busy."

"Felicia, you're not helping." Ginger already felt wracked with guilt and didn't need Felicia to add to it.

As if to backpedal, Felicia continued, "On the other hand, he has a lot more now that he's your ward. Imagine if he were still living on the streets, flea-ridden and running from the police."

"Felicia! Please."

Mallowan Court was in sight, and Ginger was grateful she could leave Felicia to her musings. She parked her motorcar with a jerk, lifting the clutch a little too soon, and hopped out of the vehicle without even closing the door behind her. Boss, sensing his mistress' anxiety, followed close on her heels.

Clement was the first person to come into view. "Have you found him? Is Scout safe?"

By the gloomy expression on her gardener's face, Ginger knew the answer before he spoke.

"No, madam. I've personally searched the garage, the stables, and the garden, but I've not found him."

Ginger was glad to hear he hadn't been discovered somewhere injured, but she did hope he'd turned up at the house since Pippins had rung. Her butler greeted her the moment she stepped inside. He answered before she had the breath to ask.

"I'm sorry, madam. No sign of him in the house. Lizzie and Grace did a thorough search."

"Oh mercy," Ginger lamented. "What on earth could've become of him?"

Ginger's heart squeezed with a pain she couldn't quite identify, then her mind went to Beatrice Edgerton and her grief. Suddenly Ginger understood. Scout Elliot was more than a ward to her. She loved him like a son; propriety be damned.

"Scout!"

The door to the sitting room was open, and Ginger rushed in. Hoping that Scout was in there was illogical, but Ginger wasn't operating out of sense. Panic propelled her. "Scout!"

"There's no need to shout."

Ginger hadn't seen Ambrosia sitting there. "Grandmother. Do you know what happened? Mrs. Beasley sent him on an errand to the Schofields next door, and it's uncertain if he returned."

"Has anyone questioned Mrs. Schofield?"

"Of course. It was the first thing Lizzie did. Clement did it for good measure too, I'm told. Quite honestly, Ginger, I'm not sure why you're so bent on helping that child. He's not one of us."

"Ambrosia!"

The Dowager Lady Gold's eyes opened wide with disbelief. Ginger was shocked herself. She'd never called her former grandmother-in-law by her Christian name before. Not to her face.

Ginger swallowed and pretended the offence had never happened. "You're not suggesting that I relinquish my responsibilities to him?"

"Certainly not. I'm only suggesting that you reassess what those responsibilities are."

"Surely, those are a moot point so long as the child is missing." Ginger pivoted on her heel and stormed out.

Boss scampered in front of her and blinked round, pitying eyes. Ginger scooped him up and buried her face into his fur. "Oh, Boss. What am I to do?"

He nuzzled his nose into her neck and let out a soft moan that sounded suspiciously like "yard."

"Of course. I must call Basil. I'm just in such a state of shock." She set Boss on the floor and raced to her study. She couldn't recall ever moving so quickly from room to room before, but the sense of urgency she felt required it.

"Basil," she said once they were connected. "I'm so glad to have caught you."

"What is it, love, is something wrong?"

"It's Scout. He's been missing since yesterday. We can't find him anywhere."

"Did you—"

"Yes. I can't believe I didn't even ask about him at breakfast this morning! Please, can you come home? I'm very worried."

"I'm on my way. I'll bring a couple of men to help with the search."

Ginger's relief was short-lived as her mind began to calculate all the possibilities. Had Scout wandered off the property and been hit by an automobile? Did he lie wounded or worse, dead, in a ditch?

Had he been kidnapped?

Ginger was an independent woman of means. Along with Hartigan House, she'd inherited half her father's American businesses which were yet thriving. Her dividends were admirable.

But Scout was her ward, legally not much more than a member of her staff as far as the public was concerned. However, anyone who knew her knew she treated her staff like family, and Scout, in particular, had a special place in her heart.

Was it someone with whom Ginger was acquainted?

Goose pimples trailed up her spine. Had she been watched? Of course. Whoever it was had monitored her comings and goings to gauge the best time to make the snatch.

Oh, where was Basil?

She found Pippins in the hallway.

"Pippins, have you noticed anyone lingering around the house? A stranger to the neighbourhood?"

Pippins shook his head. "No, madam, I can't say I have."

Enquiries with the rest of the staff produced the same result. No one had noticed anyone lurking about, and Clement was quite certain he would've spotted a stranger, especially if he'd been hanging around the alley behind the back garden.

Ginger wasn't so sure. Stealth was a concept not understood by all.

Finally, Basil made his appearance along with Sergeant Scott and Constable Braxton, who were immediately dispatched to search the grounds and surrounding streets.

"Oh, Basil, I'm just sick with worry. He's only a young boy. I'm worried someone's taken him."

Basil ushered Ginger into her study.

"Why would anyone do that?"

"For money."

Basil's brow hitched. "Ransom?"

"It must be someone who knows me," Ginger said. "Who knows I'm attached."

"Can you think of anyone?"

Ginger exhaled. "I'm quite well known in London. It could be any number of people."

"What about enemies, Ginger?" Basil asked grimly. "It's a nasty side effect of crime investigation. People get angry. Some, on occasion, may try to seek revenge."

"Madam! Madam!" Lizzie's voice reached them from the hall.

"In here, Lizzie," Ginger said. "My study." Her stomach flipped. Was Lizzie about to announce bad news?

"We've found him, madam. He just appeared in the back garden."

Ginger and Basil rushed past the maid to the back of the house. Mrs. Beasley was taking care of Scout. Or rather, he was getting a verbal beating

"Do you know how much worry you've caused the mistress? Do you think one such as yourself is worthy of the commotion you've caused?"

"It's all right, Mrs. Beasley," Ginger said.

Mrs. Beasley stepped away from Scout who looked thoroughly chastised. Ginger lowered herself onto one knee and pulled Scout into a deep embrace.

"I'm sorry, missus," he said with a sob. "I told 'im I shouldn't leave without tellin' ya."

Ginger leaned back to look into Scout's watery eyes. "Told who, Scout? Who took you?"

"Marvin, missus."

"Marvin? He's out of prison?"

"I dun't know 'ow but 'e is. Says we're family. That

we belong together. It's why 'e took me. But I told 'im I
'ad to come back to say goodbye. Proper-like."

CHAPTER TWENTY-ONE

*T*he next day was Garrett Edgerton's funeral, and as family friends, Ginger and Basil were expected to attend.

But Ginger had other ideas. If it hadn't been for her commitment to Mrs. Edgerton, she would've shadowed Scout all day on the lookout for Marvin. As it was, she'd instructed each member of the household to be diligent, and not to let Scout out of their sight. Basil was kind enough to assign Constable Braxton to stay on street watch.

Thankfully, Felicia attended the funeral as well, so Ginger didn't have to worry about her sister-in-law flaunting herself in front of the young constable.

After the funeral, the mourners were invited to the Edgertons' home for refreshments which were laid out in the drawing room, a larger version of the sitting room, but with more space around the furniture. Finger food, like small sandwiches and sliced cakes, covered tables to the side of the room. Servants walked around with trays offering various drinks.

Though there were a few people that Ginger expected—associates, friends, and members of the Edgerton family—she also recognised members of the rowing team. Though most had confessed they hadn't cared for Garrett whilst he was alive, it would've been poor form to ignore him in death. Bernard Ramsey and Howard Pritchard were in a private huddle by the window, and it was evident by the intensity of the way they were speaking, that the conversation was less than pleasant.

Basil saw her watching them and said, "I'm afraid I haven't had the chance to tell you about my latest encounter with Mr. Ramsey."

"Oh?" Ginger said with interest. "When did this happen?"

"After I dropped you off at your shop yesterday. It took me a while to run Ramsey down, but I managed to find him at a pub not far from the university. If I hadn't known better, I would have said Ramsey was intoxicated."

"Oh mercy," Ginger said. "I fear that Oliver and Matilda's esteem for Mr. Ramsey has been misplaced."

"Sadly, I have to agree. He quickly got his back up and threatened to call his solicitor."

Across the room, Bernard Ramsey abruptly turned his back on Howard Pritchard and disappeared through the crowd. Whatever they'd been discussing, it hadn't ended well. John and Jerry McMillan soon took his place. Their conversation with Mr. Pritchard appeared to be polite but boring.

Ginger scanned the room in search of the Edgertons. Oddly, Beatrice Edgerton sat alone in the far corner. With hands gloved in black lace, she held a crystal glass with what appeared to be brandy in it.

"Please excuse me, love," Ginger said to Basil. "I'm going to see how Beatrice is doing."

"And I'll look for Thurston, poor chap."

Ginger went to the grieving lady's side. "Mrs. Edgerton? Are you doing all right? I know this is a tough day for you."

Slowly, Mrs. Edgerton's head tilted upwards, and Ginger caught her dark, watery stare through her veil.

"How is our investigation progressing, Mrs. Reed?"

Ginger's gaze darted towards Basil who thankfully had found Thurston and was comfortably out of earshot. "Is this something you want to discuss here?" she asked.

In response, Beatrice's eyes went to her husband, and her frown deepened.

"No. I suppose that wouldn't be prudent. Just tell me if you've made progress. Are you any closer to finding my son's killer?"

"My investigation is active," Ginger returned vaguely. "I'll be sure to visit you next week, once things around here quieten down."

Ginger stepped away before her client could protest. What could she tell her? Her son had been unpopular and had some potential enemies? "Do take care of yourself," Ginger said kindly. "The early days are the most difficult."

Beatrice only nodded at Ginger's words of sympathy. Since the war, nearly everyone had suffered a loss of some kind.

Ginger added, "Are you sleeping all right?"

"I have today's miracle drug, Veronal. It helps me sleep and cope with my loss. It's also a deadly poison." At Ginger's startled look, she added, "Oh, don't worry, Mrs. Reed. I'm not about to take my own life."

Across the room, Bernard Ramsey topped up at a drinks trolley. A nervous fellow like that probably knew a lot more about things he wished he didn't.

"Please excuse me," Ginger said to Mrs. Edgerton, then joined the young man. "Hello, Mr. Ramsey. Good to see you again, if not for the sad circumstances."

Bernard Ramsey stared at Ginger as if he couldn't remember who she was. Ginger wasn't used to being forgotten and blamed Mr. Ramsey's poor memory on his dope habit.

"Ah, yes, Mrs. Reed. Do forgive me. This whole affair is rather distracting. I'm quite certain I'll sleep for a week once it's all over." He swallowed back the rest of the liquid in his glass.

Ginger worried for the lad. He had a hard life ahead of him if he depended on liquid courage and other stimulants to get through daily life.

"Do you not enjoy your studies?" she asked

"Not really. I'm there because my father, Sir Leonard Ramsey, is an alumnus. You don't cross Sir Leonard if you know what I mean."

Ginger didn't, but she could guess. Not all child and parent relationships were the loving sort.

"Last time we spoke, the accident had very recently happened," Ginger said. "Perhaps something new has come to mind since then." If Basil hadn't had success with his strong-handed approach, Ginger thought she might have more luck her way.

Despite Mr. Ramsey's propensity to drink, he swallowed dryly. "I'm afraid I can't think of anything."

"And you have no idea who might've wanted to harm Garrett?"

"Uh—"

They were interrupted by Howard Pritchard. "Oh, there you are, old chap!" he said. "Hey, how about leaving something for the rest of us to drink." He chuckled humorously. "Mrs. Reed. You'll have to forgive Ramsey and his tendency to be morose at the best of times. This . . ." He inclined his head. "Doesn't help."

"There's nothing to forgive."

"You don't mind if I drag the old boy away. He needs cheering up."

Mr. Ramsey's eyes darkened with distress. Perhaps Mr. Pritchard was right in taking him away. Or maybe Bernard Ramsey had been about to say something that would've implicated his friend.

CHAPTER TWENTY-TWO

*R*arely did Ginger feel the weight of exhaustion, but once it was socially acceptable to leave the Edgerton wake, she insisted on going home straightaway. She'd have even taken a hansom cab if necessary, which showed something of her determination as she usually avoided riding in any vehicle that was pulled by horses.

"I've got work to do at the office," Basil said, "but I'll drop you off first if you like."

Ginger gladly took him up on his offer.

The first matter of business on her arrival at Hartigan House was to check up on Scout. She found him in the stable with Goldmine, along with Constable Braxton, and an atypically attentive Felicia.

"Hello," Ginger said inclusively, then to Constable Braxton. "Good day, Constable."

"Good day, Mrs. Reed."

"Felicia," she began with a nod, "what brings on your sudden interest in horses?"

"I marvel at beauty no matter the medium," Felicia replied. "Goldmine is a majestic specimen."

"He's a real beauty, Mrs. Reed," Constable Braxton said. "I wouldn't have believed it if Miss Gold hadn't insisted I come to your stable to see for myself. And your boy here has a real way with the animals."

With his small palm flattened, Scout held out an apple for Goldmine to nibble on. "He's the best, missus. I would miss him so much."

Ginger's heart tightened. Oh mercy.

"Scout, perhaps we could take Boss for a little walk together."

"I'd fancy that very much, missus."

Constable Braxton cleared his throat. "I don't know if that's a good idea, madam. I promised the Chief Inspector—"

"How about you and Miss Gold follow a bit behind us." Ginger stared at Felicia, knowingly. "I suspect you'd be happy to take a bit of exercise."

"Well, I am pretty busy," Felicia said. The flirtatious twinkle in her eye was directed at Constable Braxton, who, to Ginger's dismay, looked rather besotted.

Not that Ginger would have a problem with their

pairing, but poor Ambrosia might just have a heart attack.

Felicia finally put the poor constable at ease. "But I should like a bit of fresh air."

"Very good," Constable Braxton said. "But can I suggest that we stay in the Court and not venture too far."

"Of course," Ginger said, then to Scout, "Go and find Boss and put him on a leash."

"What do you know about Marvin Elliot, Constable Braxton?" Ginger asked as they waited in the back garden and watched as Scout performed his task.

"I read his file, madam," he said. "Got involved with a bad crowd and was arrested for his part in illegal imports. Went to jail for a year, and two weeks ago got out four months early on good behaviour. His solicitor argued that his role in the Charles Derby affair had been relatively minor and that, taking Marvin's age into account, he was unduly manipulated and coerced."

Scout and Boss bounded towards them, and Ginger led the way along the side of the house to the front tall wrought iron gate. Constable Braxton lifted the latch for them to step through onto the pavement.

Ginger walked with Scout who had Boss on the leash. "Good boy," Scout said, his usual cheerful tone laced with melancholy.

"Scout," Ginger began, "you don't have to leave us, you know, even if Marvin says something different."

"But he's family."

"Aren't we family? I feel like we are."

"You do, missus? Marvin says I'm no more to you than a servant. But I don't care. I love taking care of Goldmine and Boss, even if it means having lessons and taking baths."

"Oh, Scout. You are more than a servant. You're my ward. It means I've taken legal responsibility for your wellbeing until you turn twenty-one. I don't want you to leave."

Ginger knew that she had more legal rights to Scout, but she didn't want legal rights. She wanted heart rights. She wanted Scout to stay because he wanted to, not because he was forced to.

"But what about Marvin, missus. He says he needs me."

Ginger scowled. Marvin needed Scout to help him make money on the streets. Two were better than one when it came to working a con. Yet, she felt empathy for the older boy too. Seventeen was still young to be on one's own and with no support to speak of, and now he had a criminal record.

"I'll tell you what, Scout," Ginger said. "If you agree to stay with me, I promise to help Marvin out too."

Scout grabbed Ginger in a spindly arm hug and almost caused her to lose her balance. "Thank you, missus. You are the most beautiful lady in the world."

Ginger patted the top of his newsboy cap. "There, there, Scout. Everything's going to be okay." A glance over her shoulder found the constable looking nonplus, and Felicia pouting in heartfelt sympathy.

They'd just returned to the house when Basil arrived.

Ginger knew immediately by the look on her husband's face that something was wrong.

"Basil? What is it?"

He removed his hat and held it next to his chest. "Bernard Ramsey's body has been discovered in his room by the cleaning lady."

By the time Basil and Ginger, with Boss accompanying them, arrived at the students' residence building, the police were interviewing a very shaken woman.

Basil noticed the large, lumbering body belonging to Superintendent Morris in the room, with his broad back turned. Basil exhaled, then approached.

"Superintendent?"

"Ah, Reed. You made it."

"Where's the body?" Ginger asked.

Morris stared at Ginger, who had Boss in her arms,

with distaste. He disapproved of how Basil brought her in on his investigations and didn't mind showing it. Unfortunately for Morris, Basil's bride had made herself useful to the police on more than one occasion. Morris grumbled, "In one of the upstairs bedrooms."

Ginger smiled amiably. "Superintendent Morris, so good to see you as always. You should come for dinner sometime. Mrs. Beasley is a tremendous cook."

He lumbered ahead of them going up the stairs. "Too busy for fancy dinners, Mrs. Reed."

A police constable stepped away from his position at the door when he saw them approach.

"Sirs, madam," he said.

Bernard Ramsey lay on the floor, a team scarf beside him.

Morris pointed with the toe of his large foot. "The scarf is monogrammed. Not the victim's initials."

Ginger bent down to examine the lettering. "HP." She glanced up at Basil. "Howard Pritchard?"

"A witness saw that Pritchard fellow arguing with the deceased," Morris said smugly. "My men will find him, and when they do, we'll have our killer."

"If you were going to kill someone, Superintendent," Ginger started, "would you use an item of clothing that would identify you?"

Morris snorted. "Not everyone is as bright as you, Mrs. Reed."

"She has a point, sir," Basil said. "The killer may be trying to frame Pritchard."

"It's a double bluff," Morris said. "The killer's assuming that's what we'd think."

Morris tended to jump to conclusions. It was well known that his rise to his position as superintendent had more to do with his relationship to the Lord Mayor than to actual detecting skills. Still, Basil was glad that Thurston hadn't been implicated. His friend had nothing to do with Bernard Ramsey.

Had he?

Boss sniffed the room with intent. Apparently, interesting smells came from the lad's wardrobe, his drawers, and under the bed, but it wasn't until the dog reached the headboard that he started to bark.

Morris barked back. "That creature had better not disturb the crime scene!"

Ignoring Morris, Ginger said, "What is it, Bossy?" Holding up her gloved hand for Morris to see, she then felt under the mattress and came up empty.

"My men have already checked there," Morris said smugly.

Boss sat at the corner, his stubby tail shaking with encouragement. Ginger kept digging. Basil saw the expression on her face change.

"What is it? he asked.

"There's something tucked down here. Just a

moment." Ginger's face tightened with the effort of fishing out the item. Slowly, a small tin box, the kind mints were sold in, emerged. Ginger, who was already wearing gloves, handed it to Basil who collected it carefully with a handkerchief.

Ginger gave Morris a triumphant look and scooped Boss off the floor. "Good boy, Bossy!"

Basil flipped open the lid. "White powder inside." He closed the tin and put it in a small paper evidence bag. "I'll give it to the lab."

Morris grunted, then said, "If we've finished here, the police van is waiting to take the body to the mortuary."

CHAPTER TWENTY-THREE

*G*inger hated to let Basil continue the investigation without her, but her loyalty to Mrs. Edgerton came second to her friendship with Oliver and Matilda Hill. Bernard Ramsey was one of their parishioners, and Ginger could tell by how they had supported Mr. Ramsey at the race that her friends were fond of the deceased. She wanted to be the one to give them the sad news.

Besides, they might be able to shed some light on the young man's character.

Fog had descended on London as the day drew on, and Ginger had to depend on the strength of her large round headlamps to guide her through. For once the honking horns weren't entirely directed at her.

The stones of St. George's church had darkened in the dampness giving it a ghoulish look. A stout silhouette suddenly approached, startling Ginger. Boss, whose nose wiped at the fog built up on his window, let out a low moan.

"It's okay, Boss," Ginger said lightly. "It's only Mrs. Davies."

Mrs. Davies was the church secretary and so much more. The look of consternation on the older lady's face caused Ginger to grow alarmed. She stepped out of the Crossley, Boss jumping out after her.

"Oh, Mrs. Reed. I'm so glad you're here."

"What is it, Mrs. Davies? Is something wrong?"

"It's Mrs. Hill; she's had a fall. The doctor is concerned about the baby."

Oh mercy! "Where is she? Can I see her?"

Matilda Hill had lived with Ginger for a while before she had even met Oliver Hill. An intelligent lady, Matilda had once been a student at the London Medical School for Women, but a series of events had changed her life's direction.

"She's on bed rest, madam, but I'm certain she and the reverend would be delighted to see you."

The parsonage was a quaint stone cottage that sat on the church property, and when Matilda had moved in, she had brought a cheeriness and cosiness that had been absent when Oliver lived there as a bachelor.

On hearing Ginger and Mrs. Davies enter, Oliver appeared. "Ginger! What a nice surprise."

"Mrs. Davies said Matilda has suffered a fall. Is everything all right?"

"The doctor says she's fine but wants her to rest as a precaution." Oliver made an effort to look at ease, but the hand that went to his neck confirmed the tension that Ginger sensed.

"I told her she was doing too much," Mrs. Davies said.

"Mrs. Davies has been very concerned about the child," Oliver explained. "Almost as expectant for his or her arrival as we are."

Mrs. Davies wrestled her well-worked hands. "Children are a blessing from above."

"Is she well enough for visitors?" Ginger asked.

"She'd be happy for a bit of company," Oliver replied. "As you know, Matilda's not the type who likes to be idle."

Despite being propped up in bed with her short dark hair brushed behind her ears, Matilda did look well. She was a naturally pretty girl, with wide eyes and delicate Clara Bow lips.

"My dear Matilda," Ginger said as she approached her friend. She leaned over to kiss Matilda on the forehead then took her bare hands into her own gloved ones. "You've given us all a fright."

"I only slipped one step. Bruised my behind along with my ego."

Ginger laughed. "So long as that's the only thing bruised."

Matilda smoothed the length of her nightdress over the rise of her belly. "Everything is fine. I listened to the heartbeat myself; it's nice and strong." She smiled. "I still have my stethoscope."

"How frightfully convenient! You still had another opinion, I hope."

"Oh yes. Oliver insisted we call the doctor." She smiled. "His physician agrees with me, but I'm afraid the men colluded to ensure my feet spend very little time on the floor."

"You must do what you must."

"Of course." Matilda stared questioningly at Ginger, then said, "Did you not want to have children, Ginger?"

Ginger stilled.

"I'm sorry. I can be so stupid. Forgive me. Sometimes I'm a dreadful failure in my role as sensitive vicar's wife."

Ginger patted her hand. "No, it's all right. You're doing a terrific job as vicar's wife. It's not like you can go to school to learn how. And as to your question, I very much wanted to have children. My first husband, Daniel, and I hoped for years that it would happen, but we weren't blessed in that way. Then the war happened, and we ran out of time."

"You're still young," Matilda said. "It's not too late."

Ginger forced a smile. She and Basil hadn't done anything to stop a baby from coming, yet none had. "We'll see," was all she said.

Oliver popped in with a tea tray in hand. "Mrs. Davies prepared it. I said I'd bring it in."

"Thank you, darling," Matilda said. To Ginger, she added, "Mrs. Davies means well, but since the baby, she's been rather smothering."

"I hope you don't mind if I serve the two of you," Oliver said. "I insisted that Mrs. Davies go home before she drops from exhaustion."

"That was very thoughtful of you, love," Matilda said.

Oliver added milk to the cups then poured the tea and added sugar as per Ginger and Matilda's request. Oliver pulled up an empty chair and took a seat.

"I'm afraid I have sad news for the two of you," Ginger said after a sip. "Which is the reason I came to see you. Forgive me, but I didn't know before arriving that you were resting in bed, my dear."

"How could you?" Matilda said. "What's your news?"

"It's about Bernard Ramsey. I'm afraid he's been found dead."

Oliver and Matilda shared a look of dread before

Oliver said, "Was it an overdose?"

"You knew about his problem with cocaine?" Ginger asked.

"Yes," Oliver said. "He confided in me. He desperately wanted to give up the habit, but the power of the addiction was too great."

Matilda wiped away a stray tear.

"I'm sorry to be the bearer of bad news," Ginger said kindly, "but I'm afraid it gets worse. Mr. Ramsey's death is being considered foul play."

"Foul play?" Oliver said. The fine lines around his eyes deepened. "*Murder?*"

"It appears so," Ginger said. "I'm terribly sorry."

"Is there anything you can tell me?" Oliver asked. "Some comfort I could extend to the family?"

Ginger shook her head. "I wouldn't say lest it interferes with the police investigation."

Oliver sighed as he rubbed the loose red locks off his long forehead. "I must go and call his parents."

When Oliver had left, Matilda reached for Ginger's arm. "Do they have a suspect in mind?"

Ginger thought about Howard Pritchard, how it was quite likely the police had caught up with him, and that he was now behind bars."

"Yes, love. They think they have their man."

Ginger, however, thought there was a good chance that they had the *wrong* man.

CHAPTER TWENTY-FOUR

*N*ew Scotland Yard consisted of a pair of impressive buildings of branded red brick and Portland stone, each with rounded turret corners and slanted grey slate roofs. Eager to interview Howard Pritchard, Basil made his way inside.

"He's ready for you, sir," Braxton said when he spotted Basil. "Superintendent Morris just left him."

Basil grunted. Who knew what kind of damage Morris had done? Basil always tried to interview suspects before Morris did, but sometimes his efforts failed. As expected, Pritchard was quick to come to his own defence.

"Like I told your jolly superior, I lost my scarf, all right. That makes me guilty of carelessness, nothing else."

"You're the team captain," Basil said. "Didn't your

team-mates notice that you alone were without a scarf?"

"Naturally they wouldn't let me forget it. But it's just a scarf."

"You've heard of Mr. Ramsey's demise?" Basil changed the subject.

"Yes. It's sad but not surprising. You could say Bernard lacked self-control."

"Have you—"

Pritchard interrupted. "Taken cocaine? I've got too much respect for my body to do that."

"Mr. Ramsey happened to have your scarf tied around his neck when he died," Basil said.

This time shock registered on Pritchard's face.

"And you think I did that? Left my own scarf as evidence against me? Only a fool would do such a thing."

Basil tended to agree, but responded with, "Perhaps you wanted to send a message."

"Steady on, Chief Inspector. Anyone could've taken my scarf and done that. I had no reason. I liked Ramsey, at least when he was sober. Besides, I'm rather fond of my scarf. If I did want to send a message, I'd have used another man's scarf."

"I have a witness that says you were arguing with Mr. Ramsey at Garrett Edgerton's wake."

Pritchard smirked. "Mrs. Reed? I saw her

watching us." His lips pulled up slyly. "She's a pretty bird. Nice catch, Chief Inspector. I'm fond of redheads myself."

Basil fought the sudden urge to sock this cocky upstart in the nose and responded sternly, "Keep to the point, Mr. Pritchard."

"Certainly. Anyway, it wasn't anything. Lads can fight and it not lead to murder."

"What were the two of you arguing about?"

Pritchard's arrogance took a backseat for a moment. He swallowed then said, "It was over a girl. As I said, it was nothing."

"Where were you last night, Mr. Pritchard?"

"I was in my room, studying for an exam."

"Can anyone verify that. A mate, perhaps?"

"No, I was quite alone."

Basil took a moment to scribble notes in his notebook. Often, the quiet unnerved a suspect, and they'd say something of interest to fill the void.

"Look," Pritchard finally said. "Maybe Ramsey took my scarf by mistake. It happens. The monograms are small."

"Uh-uh."

"Look here, am I under arrest?"

"The superintendent wishes for you to stay a little longer."

"Then I'm not going to say anything more without

my solicitor present. I'm innocent, I tell you. Innocent."

Basil was curious as to who Pritchard would throw to the wolves if given the chance. "Who do you think wanted to see Mr. Ramsey dead?"

Pritchard shrugged. "It could've been any of the drug users, but I'd say John and Jerry McMillan."

The McMillans? Basil had mentally crossed the twins off his list.

"What makes you think that?"

"Where do you think Ramsey got his dope from?" That stupid grin appeared on Pritchard's face again. "Cocaine doesn't just drop from the sky."

CHAPTER TWENTY-FIVE

After leaving St. George's Church, Ginger made an impulsive detour to the mortuary. An eruption of honking occurred after she skidded and made a sharp, last-moment turn. Her hand flew out to protect her dog. "Hang on, Bossy!" The fog had lifted so she couldn't very well blame the aggravation of the other drivers on it.

She changed gears to slow as she passed a policeman on his mount. There was no time to get pulled over, she thought as her mind returned to the case. Though she knew the report from Mr. Ramsey's autopsy would be sent to Scotland Yard, she believed in meeting people face to face.

The door of the mortuary was cracked open. Ginger knocked lightly.

"Dr. Gupta?"

The mortuary appeared empty. How odd for the door to be open and unlocked. Perhaps he was at his desk in the office? That door was also propped open.

The reason that Dr. Gupta hadn't heard her call out was that he was occupied. Ginger jumped out of sight and held in a yelp. Dr. Gupta was busy, all right, busy kissing his wife!

Ginger felt like a terrible peeping Tom.

She was about to knock when she saw him lay a hand on Mrs. Gupta's stomach. It bulged slightly, as though she was in the family way. Ginger's feeling of envy stunned her. Dr. Gupta had only brought his bride to London from India the previous spring. It seemed that everyone other than Ginger was blessed with a child.

Boss yipped, and Ginger felt herself redden with embarrassment.

"I beg your pardon," she said. "The door was open. I called out—"

The Guptas jumped apart, and Mrs. Gupta smoothed out her shiny silk sari, and pushed a long black braid over her shoulder.

"Hello, Mrs. Reed."

"I'm so sorry to interrupt."

"It's fine," Dr. Gutpa said. "I'm at work. Working." He cleared his throat. "My wife just brought me a flask of Indian chai."

"I was on my way out," Mrs. Gupta said. "I'll see you at home later, Dr. Gupta."

Dr. Gupta grinned at his wife. "Goodbye, love." Then in a most professional manner, he turned to Ginger. "What can I do for you, Mrs. Reed?"

"Again, I do apologise—"

"Don't mention it."

"I wonder if you have the autopsy report for Mr. Ramsey ready? I know the body only came in last night."

"I arrived bright and early to perform the post-mortem at the superintendent's request. The report is ready and in the post to the police."

"Is there something of note, Dr. Gupta? Was the cause of death strangulation?" Killers had been known to play with the police in the past, and it wouldn't have been beyond the realms of possibility that Mr. Ramsey had died another way and the scarf placed afterwards as a ruse.

"As a matter of fact, the hyoid bone was intact."

So Ginger's hunch had been correct.

"I found evidence of recent cocaine use in the victim's nostrils."

"He was a known user. Perhaps this was an overdose and not foul play at all?" What a relief that would be to Oliver and Matilda, Ginger thought, along with Mr. Ramsey's family.

"Perhaps. The toxicology tests are underway. I already promised Chief Inspector Reed that I'd ring him when they came in."

Dr. Gupta looked at Ginger but was too polite to ask her why she was at the mortuary asking questions that the police, her own husband, would be informed about. Ginger couldn't very well tell the pathologist that she was working separately on the case for a private client. It was all a bit redundant. Once again, she regretted allowing Mrs. Edgerton to talk her into it.

"Marvellous," Ginger said benignly. "Thank you, Doctor." She patted the thigh of her pleated Parisian skirt. "Come along, Boss."

Ginger strolled away without looking back, hoping that this unfortunate interruption would soon be forgotten by all.

CHAPTER TWENTY-SIX

*B*asil hoped to save time by using the newly installed candlestick telephone in his office at Scotland Yard. He'd welcomed the contraption when it was first put in, especially now that most institutions and some homes boasted of having at least one. They were dashed useful.

The first place he rang was the University of London, and after a long wait—during which time Basil swore he could've actually driven there—the senior tutor was finally found.

"I hope I haven't inconvenienced you too terribly," Basil said, "but I have to enquire after John and Jerry McMillan. Do you know their whereabouts?"

A heavy sigh reached Basil from the other end. "Just a moment, Chief Inspector, whilst I check the timetable."

Basil's impatience made his skin feel as if it were tightening, along with every internal organ. Something had to break in the Garrett case soon. Blast it! He couldn't face Thurston and Beatrice again if the case went cold.

"Chief Inspector?"

"Yes?"

"It appears that the lads have cut their timetabled lecture."

"Are you saying you don't know where they are?"

"I can't say for certain, but you might try the Thames." The senior tutor hung up before Basil could question him further.

The Thames? That was a mighty long river.

Basil grabbed his hat and coat, stopping briefly to let the officer at the desk know where he was going, then headed to the car park and got into his Austin. If the Thames was his destination, he simply had to cross the road as the Yard sat across the street from the Victoria Embankment. However, the university's boat club was a better guess, and Basil headed in that direction.

The club was unlocked. An act of carelessness, Basil thought, considering no one appeared to be on the premises to answer his knock.

"Hello," he said, as he walked in. "Scotland Yard, here."

He carefully trod across the wooden floor, the soft soles of his shoes hardly making a sound. The meeting room was empty, though not exactly tidy, with rowing magazines askew on the coffee table, empty beer bottles, and full ashtrays.

The floor above creaked, and Basil's attention shot upward. The attic, where bedrooms had been constructed for the building's former owners, a club now defunct that had come from outside London.

All the oarsmen had rooms at the Imperial Institute. So who was upstairs?

Treading as lightly as possible, Basil crept up the stairs. The closer he got to the top, the louder the voices became.

Male.

McMillan.

"I told you we're moving too fast!"

"Hold it together, Jerry. We need to wait a bit."

Basil astounded them as he entered the room at the top of the stairs. "Good afternoon, gentlemen."

"Ch-chief Inspector," one of them muttered.

Small scar left temple.

"Hello, John," Basil said.

John pointed to his head. "So you noticed it, eh? I suppose a keen eye is necessary in your profession."

Ginger was the one who had noticed it, but Basil didn't want to bring attention to her. He had a feeling this encounter might get ugly. He walked over to the mattress that Jerry had unceremoniously sat upon and pressed his hand along the surface.

"Rather bumpy, isn't it?" Basil said. "I don't suppose it's too comfortable to sleep on."

"Good thing no one sleeps up here," John said.

"What are you good fellows doing up here?"

John was definitely the mouthpiece of the two. "I might ask the same of you."

"I'm on police business." Basil didn't like the fact that they outnumbered him, and that these lads were half his age and twice as fit. A good bluff was in order. "My officers are on their way. What do you think they'll find here?"

Jerry's eyes widened with dread as his gaze shot to his brother's. "I'm not going to jail, John."

"Shut up, you idiot."

"I had nothing to do with this," Jerry said. Before Basil could lay a hand on him to stop him, Jerry sprang to his feet and darted down the steps.

Basil blocked John's way. "Looks like you and Jerry will be seeing each other in prison."

John McMillan snarled. "Not if I have anything to do with it."

Basil expected the attack when it came and immediately found himself in a wrestling lock hold. Basil might have been older, but he'd also been in the ring a few more times than John.

The wrestling match pushed the men up against the wall, through the bedroom door, and onto the landing dangerously close to the staircase.

"You're adding aggravated assault of a police officer to your charge, Mr. McMillan," Basil muttered with loss of breath.

With renewed vigour John McMillan thrust Basil toward the step. Losing his footing, Basil caught the rail, preventing his fall. John took the opportunity to leap over Basil's body and run down the steps.

Basil roused himself to go after him. John had disappeared around the bend at the bottom landing, and Basil nearly tripped over his body where he lay, curled in a ball, holding his head in pain.

Braxton stood over him with his truncheon lifted. Then he smiled at Basil.

"Sergeant Scott sent me. He rang the university looking for you and was told, based on your recent telephone call to them, that you might be here. He thought you might need a bit of help."

Basil gained control of his breathing. He owed Scott a pint.

CHAPTER TWENTY-SEVEN

Ginger was exhausted by the end of the day and eagerly accepted the offer of an evening brandy to share with Basil in the sitting room. This case was proving to be a complicated affair for both the Yard and Lady Gold Investigations.

"Pippins," she said as he approached with two drinks atop a silver platter. "You are an angel."

"It's my pleasure, madam."

She cuddled up close to Basil with her legs stretching out along the length of the settee. Boss curled up by her toes.

"Tell me again what you learned today?" It was an innocent question, except for the fact that she was asking it on behalf of her client and not merely as a matter of curiosity.

"Pritchard denies having anything to do with

Ramsey's death and claims his scarf went missing. It was Morris' idea to bring him in on circumstantial evidence, and he's a bear now for having had to release his only suspect."

"You did warn him," Ginger said.

"I think he hoped to break Pritchard into confessing. Unfortunately for Morris, Pritchard clammed up and rang for his solicitor."

"An intelligent man would do no less."

"However, Pritchard did implicate the McMillan twins."

"Oh, how so?"

"He suggested that they supplied the cocaine to Ramsey."

"Oh mercy. Well, I imagine it has to come from somewhere. Is it true?"

"Er, I had an unfortunate encounter with them earlier. They're locked up, but refusing to talk."

Ginger's heart skipped a beat. Basil had got himself into life-threatening situations before, and it would've been two against one with the twins. "You weren't in danger, were you?"

"I found them at the boat club. I got into a bit of a scuffle with John McMillan, but I'm fine. Braxton proved his mettle."

"I'm glad to hear it turned out in your favour," Ginger said. "I'm sure Felicia would be thrilled to hear about Constable Braxton's heroics."

Basil chuckled. "I'll entertain her with the tale sometime."

"What I don't understand is why they would want to kill Bernard? It's like killing a repeat customer. Hardly good for the bank balance."

"Maybe he could no longer pay," Basil said. "That's what these insidious dealers do. They continue to raise the price as the addict's needs intensify."

"But dead, he can never pay. It's lost income."

"True."

"And what about Garrett?" Ginger asked. "The brothers had an alibi—each other, mind you, and no motive to speak of."

"That we know of."

"Yes, however, I'm inclined to believe that we're looking at two different crimes. Drug trafficking and manslaughter."

Basil hitched a brow. "Not murder?"

"At the moment, no." Ginger sipped her drink then looked at Basil. "I visited Dr. Gupta today, and he confirmed that Mr. Ramsey hadn't died as a result of strangulation. His death is quite possibly accidental."

Basil exhaled. "We still don't know who dunked Garrett, or where it happened."

"Not all the laboratory results have come in, have

they?" Ginger said. "Maybe something new shall come to light."

"I do hope so. For Thurston and Beatrice's sakes."

Ginger sipped her brandy and took a fortifying breath. She wanted to discuss another unrelated topic with her husband.

"Actually, love, I did learn something else from my visit to the mortuary."

"Yes?"

"Dr. Gupta and his wife are in the family way."

"Really? How do you know that?"

"I overheard something they said. To be truthful, it was rather awkward."

"Well, good for them."

He twisted slightly to look at her face. "You don't seem very happy for them."

"Oh, I am. It's just—" The emptiness she felt brought a sadness she could no longer contain. "Oh, Basil."

Basil stroked her hair and kissed her head. "I know."

Ginger decided to dive right in. "What about adoption?"

"Adoption?"

"Yes. Would you consider it, Basil?"

Ginger felt Basil stiffen and held her breath.

"Sorry, darling," Basil finally said. "I didn't expect that."

"Are you saying you've never thought about it?"

"I can honestly say I have not. But seriously, Ginger, do consider how disruptive a newborn would be to our lives. Your life. You have your shop, and don't forget about Lady Gold Investigations. You couldn't very well solve crimes with an infant on your hip."

"I'd employ a nanny, love. Anyway, it's a good thing I'm not considering an infant."

Ginger pulled away and turned to face him, nearly knocking Boss to the floor with her feet. He responded by giving Ginger a look of reproach before leaping to the floor and slinking to his bed by the fire.

Basil walked to the sideboard and topped up his drink. "I'm afraid I'm not following."

"What if we didn't adopt a baby, but a child of say, eleven?"

Basil narrowed his gaze. "You're not suggesting—"

"What if I am? Would it be so terrible?"

"It's just not done."

"Oh, shucks," Ginger jumped defiantly to her feet. "In this instance, I'm throwing out my ties to British propriety and wearing my American heritage proudly. I don't care if something's *not done*. I'll do it anyway!"

Basil's resistance softened, and his lips curled up. "I do adore you when you get feisty."

"Basil, I'm serious."

"I can see that. So, you're saying you want to adopt Scout officially?"

"I do."

"But he already lives with us. His life has very much improved since we first met him on the SS *Rosa*."

"Yes, but we can give him a name and a future. We can give him *parents*."

Basil emptied his glass. "I see you've put a lot of thought into this already. Can we at least sleep on it for a few nights?"

Ginger sashayed over to her husband, loosened his tie, and then whispered in his ear. "Are you sure you want to *sleep*?"

Basil swooped her up into his arms. She laughed as he carried her up the staircase to their bedroom, quite ignoring certain members of the staff who pretended not to notice.

CHAPTER TWENTY-EIGHT

The next morning, the papers announced the arrest of the McMillan brothers and rambled on about the streak of bad luck happening to the rowing team. Two deaths and now drugs.

Ginger scoured the newsprint over breakfast but found nothing new there that she didn't already know.

Felicia sprang into the morning room with the energy of a colt, and Ginger arched a brow in question.

"What's got into you?"

"Why?" Felicia feigned a pout. "Can't a girl just be happy in the morning?"

Upon hearing Felicia's voice, Lizzie entered the room. "I have a fresh pot of tea, miss? Shall I pour for you?"

Felicia nodded. "Yes, please."

Determined, Ginger tried to get to the bottom of

Felicia's uncharacteristic burst of morning energy before Ambrosia arrived and squashed Felicia's flow of words.

"Felicia? Is that new perfume I smell?"

"Oh, perhaps," Felicia said with a mischievous twinkle in her eye. "I'm going for a morning stroll through Kensington Gardens. So lovely this time of year, don't you agree? The tulip beds are darling!"

Boss sat eagerly beside Ginger's chair—Ginger admitted it was a bad habit she'd allowed both of them to fall into. It was at breakfast only, mind you. She offered Boss a small piece of sausage that disappeared faster than a blink then wiped her fingers on the napkin that lay across her lap.

"Your gentleman friend wouldn't happen to be an actual *gentleman* of the genteel world, would he?"

"Ginger! You are the last person I would expect to be snobbish. Haven't you just married *down*?"

"Yes, but I don't have Ambrosia to deal with."

"Lucky for you."

"If she finds out, your murder will be the next case I'll be solving. You wouldn't want to see your grandmother put behind bars, would you?"

Felicia sniffed. "Stop being so dramatic. We're only going on a stroll through the park. It's not like we're eloping."

Thank goodness for small miracles, Ginger

thought. "I'm needed at the shop," she said. Then with an arched brow directed Felicia's way she added, "Oh, did I give you the day off? I don't recall doing that."

"Hilarious, Mrs. Reed. I'll be in later; don't worry."

Ginger pushed away from the table knowing she'd never win a verbal battle with her sister-in-law. As she left, she said with a smile, "Say hello to Constable Braxton for me."

Basil had left early for the Yard. Ginger saw that the intensifying of this case, with no resolution in sight, was getting to her husband. The best thing she could do was to give him time to himself. She had her own business to attend to, as it was.

As Ginger parked along the kerb around the corner from her Regent Street shop, she noticed a "To Let" sign hanging in the window of the small shoe repair business next door. In a hurry to get to work, she didn't have time to consider the implications.

The busiest times of the year for dress shops across Europe happened in spring and autumn as fashionable ladies of a certain status wanted to add the latest designs to their wardrobes. It wasn't startling for Ginger to see the shop buzzing with ladies since the latest advert had gone out.

Oh mercy. She should've insisted that Felicia come in immediately. Somehow that girl always managed to get her way, especially where her romantic fancies came into play.

Fortunately, Madame Roux, always reliable, and Dorothy were proficient at keeping the customers happy. Emma worked on the shop floor as well when the need arose.

As she walked into the shop, Ginger, with a raised voice, said, "Ladies. Welcome to Feathers & Flair. Please allow one of us to cater to your every need." Ginger assisted a particularly demanding customer, which ended, thankfully, with a satisfactory sale sure to be a boon to the shop's financial success.

"Thank you, Lady Clementine," Ginger said as she handed the lady several bags.

Dorothy had a free moment and carried out the hatboxes to Lady Clementine's vehicle and driver.

The bell above the door rang, and Ginger's focus immediately darted to the new customer. She worked to keep the jolt she felt from registering on her face.

"Mrs. Edgerton?"

It hadn't even been a week since the poor lady had lost her son. Seeing as she was in mourning, she was hardly there to shop for new clothes, but perhaps she needed something else in black.

"Hello, Mrs. Reed," Mrs. Edgerton started. "I was just in the area. . . I couldn't stand sitting around at home a moment longer. . . I hoped to find you here."

"It's quite all right, Mrs. Edgerton. A little diversion is necessary once in a while."

As serendipity would have it, at that moment Felicia fluttered in like a dove, her eyes twinkling with joy.

"I take it your stroll went well?" Ginger said.

"Swimmingly!"

"I can't wait to hear all about it, later. If you don't mind jumping in, there are customers here waiting for your assistance."

Felicia's balloon couldn't be popped, and she practically floated to the back room to discard her hat and gloves.

"I do apologise, Mrs. Edgerton."

"I understand. It's hard to find good workers these days."

Ginger smirked. "Indeed. Now, how can I help you?"

"I probably shouldn't have come in. I see you are very busy."

"No, it's fine. I've got enough girls working now."

Through Mrs. Edgerton's veil, Ginger could see a look of hope flash across her eyes. "I only wondered if perhaps you'd learned anything new?"

Ginger thought back to everything that had happened since she'd last met with her client. "Perhaps we should go outside where we can talk more freely."

"Of course."

The pleasant weather had brought out more shoppers. Businessmen in summer suits and trilby hats hurried about instead of taking a hansom cab or driving themselves. Pedestrians going in all directions crowded the pavement. The noise of passing lorries and the clopping of horseshoes on cobblestones filled the air along with the call of sales boys shouting as they pitched their wares. A nanny pushed a baby in a pram past them, and they had to step out of the way to make room for the contraption's large wheels.

It was the perfect place for a private conversation.

"Have you spoken to the police recently?" Ginger asked once they'd moved away from the shop.

"Thurston won't let me in on those conversations," Mrs. Edgerton replied. "He says they'll only upset me, but what he doesn't understand is that not knowing is far worse."

"I'm sorry to say that another young man has died since I last saw you at your son's wake," Ginger said. "You've probably heard?"

"Yes, Thurston did find it appropriate to tell me that much. Better from him than the paper, he said." She clucked her tongue, then added, "Poor Mr. Ramsey."

Ginger knew that the police hadn't released news about the scarf found around Mr. Ramsey's neck, and she kept that titbit to herself. Instead, she said, "We think it's possible that a member of the rowing team might be involved."

"I'm not surprised. My Garrett was a talented athlete and a credible threat to anyone who might've wanted to challenge him in the future."

Ginger was taken aback by the force behind Beatrice Edgerton's words.

"My husband may not tell me much, Mrs. Reed," Mrs. Edgerton continued, "but I did overhear one particular telephone conversation of interest."

"Oh?"

"My husband was talking to Mrs. Ainsley."

"The coach's wife?"

"Yes."

"You and she are friends, are you not?"

"Well, I suppose I should admit our friendship has become strained over the last year."

Ginger had the feeling Beatrice Edgerton wanted to tell her why. It would be imprudent for her to ask outright, so she waited for the silence to build.

Mrs. Edgerton broke it. "I'm sure this has nothing to do with the tragic events that have unfolded, but I think, as an investigator, you should be aware of all the forces at work. Mrs. Ainsley, as you know, is a young lady much younger than her husband and quite a bit younger than me. A decade at least, but that didn't seem to matter at the beginning. We were both married women of a certain social circle.

"However, it turns out that Carol fancies the younger lot, young men." She eyed Ginger from under her veil. "I'm sure you understand my full meaning."

"And you think she was involved with members of the rowing team?"

"I don't think, Mrs. Reed. I know. She confided in me that she has a studio over the mews, separate from the house she shares with Mr. Ainsley. He was married once before, and she was his mistress. He bought her the studio for their trysts. She told him she needed to keep it as a studio for her artwork—she considers herself to be a top-notch watercolour painter, but she's an amateur at best, I can assure you. But I know for a fact that she entertains there, without her husband. Forgive me for being so vulgar, except that the circumstances appear to require it."

As far as scandals went, Ginger had heard far worse. "And she uses this studio to entertain members of the rowing teams?"

"Quite. It's her den of iniquity, you could say. Poor hapless lads. It pains me terribly to say it, but my Garrett fell prey to her seduction."

Ginger thought back to the boat club party and recalled the look of intimacy that had flashed between them. She'd thought it simple flirting at the time.

Ginger felt a surge of sympathy for this mother.

"It might help you to know that Mr. Ramsey was among them," Mrs. Edgerton said.

Ginger shuddered to a stop. "Are you saying she killed—"

Beatrice Edgerton put a gloved hand on Ginger's arm and spoke softly into her ear. "Carol Ainsley may be what is maliciously referred to in foreign films as a *black widow*."

CHAPTER TWENTY-NINE

Ginger decided to call on Mrs. Ainsley after Beatrice Edgerton had given her the address of her fellow redhead's studio. It was quite possible that Carol Ainsley would be at her marital home, but Ginger's curiosity pushed her to see this "den of iniquity."

The top-floor studio was located in an obscure mews in Hammersmith.

Ginger, with Boss on her heels, climbed the staircase, then knocked tentatively on the door. She waited, rapped again, and was about to give up when the door cracked open. Carol Ainsley stood on the other side of the threshold wearing an afternoon frock sewn from sensual deep-purple crepe satin with bold, contrasting aqua-blue accents. She had one carefully manicured hand on a hip whilst the other held an ivory cigarette holder with a half-burned cigarette glowing red from the end.

"Mrs. Reed," Carol Ainsley said staidly. "This is a surprise."

Ginger scooped Boss into her arms. "Might I come in? I promise my pet is well behaved."

Mrs. Ainsley eyed Boss with indifference. "Very well." She sashayed down a narrow corridor and through a set of open French glass doors into the main room.

Indian carpets covered the floors, silk lamps trimmed with tassels stood close to luxurious chairs and an overstuffed sofa, and garish paintings hung on the wall. Her own work? Ginger had been told that Mrs. Ainsley was an artist, and this was evident by the paint supplies and sketchpads covering a tall table. An easel faced the wall making it impossible for Ginger to see what curious drawing might be etched on the other side.

"I understand you are a painter," Ginger said politely.

"I dabble. It's a hobby, nothing more."

The studio smelled thickly of cigarettes, and Ginger held a gloved hand over her lips to stifle a cough. Mrs. Ainsley did her no favours when she inhaled and blew out a long blue stream of smoke.

Carol Ainsley fell graciously into one of the chairs,

then instructed, "Have a seat." A decanter and one crystal glass sat on the small table beside her. "I know it's a little early for brandy, but under the circumstances, I'm going to have a nip. Shall I get you a glass?"

"No, thank you." Ginger accepted the proffered chair and placed Boss on her lap. "I expect I won't be long."

Mrs. Ainsley held her gaze. "Pity. It's been so lonely since, well, all this frightful business."

Ginger noted how her hostess' hand shook as she poured herself a glass of what appeared to be whisky. Ginger suspected that this wasn't the lady's first drink of the day.

"Your husband doesn't mind that you're here?"

Mrs. Ainsley shrugged her partially bare shoulder. "He's always at work, so what does it matter to him. So long as I'm home by seven. It's not like he tracks my every step. At least—"

She stopped to take a drag of her cigarette. "At least, not until Harry."

Harry Brooks, the young man who had lost his place on the rowing team.

"So the rumours were true?" Ginger said.

"What can I say? I love men."

"I understand you had a . . . er . . . friendship with Bernard Ramsey."

"Oh, that poor boy. I can't believe he's dead!" Mrs. Ainsley took another large sip of her whisky.

Were the dramatics put on as a disguise for guilt? Ginger wondered. Or was she sincerely sorry and speaking out of her slightly intoxicated state?

Ginger dared to venture, "Did your husband know about him?"

Carol tapped ashes into a tray then stubbed out her cigarette. She took another sip of her drink.

"You must think me very vile, Mrs. Reed. And perhaps I am a little wicked. But I promised Jasper that I'd stop with Harry Brooks, and I have. Or at least I'm trying. But Howard can be a stubborn brute."

Ginger raised a brow. "Howard Pritchard?"

"Mrs. Reed, you're a beautiful redhead, like me. I know you capture the eyes of men of all ages. I've seen them looking at you myself. Don't tell me it doesn't tempt you."

"Mrs. Ainsley, I can assure you that the colour of our hair is the only thing we have in common on this count. I'm not naive enough to deny that I don't turn heads, but one only has to resist the temptation for it to leave."

Carol Ainsley wiggled her fingers weakly. "Oh, you're still in your honeymoon stage. Wait until your husband is so busy with work that he forgets that he's married. Or worse, he's got another little something set up on the side."

So that was the root of Carol Ainsley's angst, Ginger thought. Mr. Ainsley wasn't innocent when it came to marital betrayal. Such an unhappy arrangement. Ginger suddenly felt pity for the lady.

"What about John and Jerry McMillan?" Ginger asked. "Are they also guests of yours?"

"I'm afraid they're not my type, though they do have their uses."

"Cocaine?"

"I have no idea what you're talking about, darling." Carol Ainsley put on a theatrical air

"Mrs. Ainsley, have you ever had Mr. Pritchard's scarf?"

The change in subject caused Mrs. Ainsley to sit upright. "Why would you ask me that?"

"Has Mr. Pritchard left his scarf behind?"

Having found her composure, Ginger's hostess relaxed into her chair. "Such an odd question, Mrs. Reed. The answer is no. One thing I've learned is to never, ever leave evidence behind. I make sure my visitors leave with everything they came with." The corner of her mouth twitched upwards. "You'll remember to take your dog with you when you go, won't you?"

$\mathcal{G}$inger decided it was time to visit Basil at Scotland Yard.

"I had two interesting encounters this afternoon," Ginger said once she was seated in Basil's office. She relayed her encounter with Mrs. Edgerton and her subsequent visit with Mrs. Ainsley.

"Beatrice suggested that Carol Ainsley might be responsible for Mr. Ramsey's death?" Basil said.

"She called Mrs. Ainsley 'a black widow'. Though Carol Ainsley's not technically a widow, I believe the sentiment is that she's a female who preys on the weakness of men."

"My word." Basil tented his fingers and raised them to his chin. "And now that you've had your *tête-à-tête* with Mrs. Ainsley, do you agree?"

"Carol Ainsley is a tormented lady, and I don't

envy her," Ginger said. "And it is interesting that she's been involved with both victims and two of our prime suspects, Brooks and Pritchard."

"Yes," Basil said dourly. "And we don't have evidence to hold either one of them."

Ginger, unable to find a word of encouragement regarding their case, offered the next pressing item on her mind. "Do you know that Constable Braxton is walking out with Felicia?"

Basil jerked in his chair. "What? No!"

"It's true. They went for a stroll through Kensington Gardens just this morning."

"Shall I put a stop to it?"

"Does your authority over the constable extend to his private life?"

"Only if his personal affairs are criminal."

"His daring with Felicia isn't illegal, though I'm sure Ambrosia would beg to differ." Ginger mimicked the elderly lady, "Society has its own set of laws."

"If it's any consolation, Brian Braxton came to us with excellent references. I do believe he's a man of good character."

"That does ease my mind a great deal, Basil. It's best we both stay out of Felicia's affairs. She'd never forgive me if I meddled, and who knows, they could end up a happy pairing."

"It's a little early to draw any conclusions, I expect."

Ginger startled at a tap on the door which opened to reveal the constable.

Basil remained calm. "Constable?"

"I'm sorry to interrupt, sir, but the fingerprinting report on Mr. Ramsey's mint tin has come in. There are only two sets identified—one belonging to Mr. Ramsey and the other to Mr. Howard Pritchard."

Ginger and Basil shared a look. Finally!

"Thank you, Constable. Have you been able to locate the whereabouts of Mr. Pritchard?"

"We're working on it, sir."

Once Constable Braxton had left, Basil said, "Pritchard and Ramsey were both connected to Carol Ainsley, and consequently, both had access to cocaine. Together they held Garrett underwater, each for their own reasons still yet to be determined." He lifted a shoulder. "It's a good theory."

"Perhaps Mr. Ramsey wanted to confess," Ginger added, "and Mr. Pritchard found a way to stop him."

Basil circled his desk and kissed Ginger on the lips. "I love it when you talk crime."

Ginger laughed and pushed him away. "Go and get your suspect."

. . .

GINGER FELT it was her duty to inform her client of her latest findings and drove across the city to the Edgerton manor. She felt quite pleased with herself. She was able to honour her client's wishes without violating Basil's trust.

There was a particular thrill that came with closing a case, though Ginger had to give most of the credit for this one to Basil and Scotland Yard. Beatrice Edgerton hadn't gained anything more from employing Ginger than she would've done by sitting patiently whilst the police did their work.

Ginger mightn't even have accepted payment if it weren't for the fact that the Edgertons were quite able to pay. Proceeds from her work for Lady Gold Investigations went to the Child Wellness Project she and Reverend Hill had set up in aid of London's street children. Beatrice Edgerton could be comforted by the fact that her fee was going to a good cause.

After the long tone of the bell and some moments before the butler answered the heavy door, Ginger was ushered into the drawing room. Shortly afterwards, Mrs. Edgerton, dressed fashionably in black, joined her.

"Mrs. Reed. I gather you have something new to report?"

"I do, Mrs. Edgerton. You'll be pleased to know that an arrest is about to be made."

A slight gasp was followed by, "Who?"

"Howard Pritchard."

"Howard?" Mrs. Edgerton lowered herself onto the settee. "But Howard and Garrett were like brothers once. 'Live together, die together,' they used to say. You know how fanciful children can be."

Beatrice Edgerton had grown pale, and Ginger worried about her well-being. "Shall I ring for tea?"

"Yes, of course. I should've offered."

Ginger found the bell on the wall and pushed the button. A maid ducked in, and Ginger requested the tea.

An uncomfortable silence settled, and Ginger searched for something appropriate to say. "I hope this news brings the peace you've been seeking."

Mrs. Edgerton stared back at Ginger with blank eyes. "It does, Mrs. Reed. Thank you."

CHAPTER THIRTY-ONE

When Ginger got back to Hartigan House she rewarded herself with a cup of coffee laced with a dollop of brandy. Enjoying the privacy of her study, she leaned back in her leather chair and put her feet up on the desk. Solving a case always came with a profound sense of accomplishment and a warm feeling of euphoria. She stared at Boss, who was curled up in front of the fire that now blazed thanks to Lizzie's efforts.

"We did it again, Bossy."

She let out a satisfied sigh and studied the photograph of her father in his youth, which hung from picture wire on the wall. She wondered what he'd have thought of her new work as a private investigator? Her business cards had arrived and stood in a neat pile, each with shiny embossed gold script that read:

Lady Gold Investigations

Her mind recalled her other business, Feathers & Flair, and for a moment she wondered if perhaps she'd taken on too much. Especially in light of her objectives for young Scout.

However, her heart beat equally strongly for all three of those endeavours, and she decided that she didn't have to *choose,* she just had to *manage.* One thing she'd learned well during her work in the Great War was the necessity to plan and organise, to prioritise, and when necessary, change direction. Feathers & Flair could run, for the most part, without her being present in the shop every day. Her household matters were well under control with Pippins in charge, and Lizzie was a capable nanny for Scout. Even without an official adoption, Ginger already functioned in the role of mother, seeing to it that Scout had access to the necessities of life, an education, and her loving arms.

Lady Gold Investigations could use more structure. At the moment, potential clients had to ring her at home, or worse, drop in to Feathers & Flair. That wasn't professional at all.

She thought of the little space next to her shop that had come up for rent.

Of course! That was the answer. A quick search through the telephone book provided the phone number she needed. Within minutes, she'd completed the transaction. The papers would be couriered over in the morning for her signature!

Ginger could imagine the sign over the door and the convenience of an office next to Feathers & Flair. She could move into the space at the end of the month, and Felicia could help her to decorate. After all, Felicia had proved to have excellent taste when Hartigan House needed a fresh look.

Ginger had a sudden desire to share all her news with someone. She wondered when Basil would be home and checked her watch. Surely, the arrest of Howard Pritchard had occurred by now?

She quickly tidied her desk then called for Boss. "Let's see if we can find Felicia, shall we?"

Boss was immediately up to the task, and the sound of his nails tapped against the marble flooring. "We'll have to see if Clement can cut your nails again, old boy."

Ginger found Felicia in the sitting room where she reclined on the settee looking rather dejected. She sniffed when Ginger walked in. "The shop was frightfully busy. I don't think I sat down for a minute. My feet disliked the matter very much. I don't know if my toes shall recover." She wiggled them beneath her stockings for effect.

"It's a busy time of year. Things will slow down after a while."

"And where did you disappear to?" Before Ginger could respond, she continued with her complaint. "It must be nice to be the boss of the show. I'd rather like to be the owner of something and just make commands all day. 'Do this, I say. Do that.'"

Ginger laughed. "Oh, Felicia, you are the best. One day it will surely come to pass."

Felicia emitted a loud sigh. "Not by writing, I declare."

"Oh dear." Ginger commiserated. "Not another rejection?"

"The evening post came with another letter from some obscure publisher. I'm not even meriting the appreciation of small fish."

"What did the letter say?"

"I don't know. I haven't opened yet."

"You haven't opened it?"

"I can't bear to. I can't bear another rejection."

Ginger spied the unopened envelope on the coffee table.

"Is that it? Would you like me to open it for you?"

"Would you? I'd be grateful. Break it to me gently, please."

Ginger smiled. "Very well." She reached for the envelope and raised a brow. "Mr. Frankie Gold?"

"I gave myself a man's name this time," Felicia explained. "I believe the other publishers rejected me strictly based on my gender. As if the female species doesn't have an imagination! We have the wildest imagination of all!"

Ginger laughed. "Well, *you* certainly do."

"Are you going to read it?"

"Yes." Ginger scanned the letter and perceived the contents. She cleared her throat and enjoyed the moment to tease Felicia and extend her anticipation.

"Dear Mr. Gold,

We are pleased to inform you that your manuscript meets our approval and would be pleased to discuss publication."

The room filled with Felicia's voice as she squealed in pleasure. No longer did she complain about sore feet as she pranced excitedly around the room.

"They like it. They like it! Ginger, I'm going to be a published author!"

Ginger found herself on her feet as well. She embraced Felicia and joined in the impromptu dance.

"Congratulations! I'm so happy for you."

"Thank you, Ginger!"

"I only wish now you'd let me read it."

"Oh, you'd love the extraordinary ending! What happens is—"

Before Ginger could stop her from spoiling the

ending, Felicia spouted, "The client is the killer! The person who employed my detective is the murderer. He only wanted help in finding his next victim. Isn't that fabulous?"

The room felt as if it were spinning, and Ginger felt herself go pale. Her knees turned to jelly as she lowered herself into a chair. She heard Felicia's voice on the periphery. "Ginger? Are you all right?"

Call it poetic justice.

Was that why Beatrice Edgerton had asked for her help?

Don't worry, Mrs. Reed. I'm not about to take my own life.

Had she been hinting that she intended to take the life of the person she felt was responsible for Garrett's death?

Howard and Garrett were like brothers once, you know. Live together, die together they used to say.

Oh mercy!

Beatrice Edgerton was going to kill Howard Pritchard, and Ginger had led her straight to him!

CHAPTER THIRTY-TWO

*T*he telephone receiver was hot in Ginger's hand when she dialled Scotland Yard. "Please, connect me to Chief Inspector Basil Reed. It's urgent!"

She paced as she waited.

Sensing Ginger's anxiety, Boss whimpered.

A strange voice answered. "Chief Inspector Reed is not at his desk. Would you like to leave a message?"

Of course, he wouldn't be there. He was out looking for Howard Pritchard.

"I'd like to speak to Superintendent Morris, please. Tell him it's important."

Ginger and the superintendent rarely saw eye to eye, but she hoped he would see past his prejudice and listen to her. It seemed like forever before the burly man finally answered the telephone.

"Morris speaking."

"Superintendent Morris, it's Georgia Reed."

"Mrs. Reed, we're swamped—"

"Please, I think Howard Pritchard's life is in danger."

"It's my understanding that he's the one endangering life."

"I'm afraid we may have got it wrong, sir. I believe Mrs. Edgerton might be seeking revenge. I think she killed Bernard Ramsey too."

"Why would you think that, Mrs. Reed."

"Superintendent, has the toxicology report on Mr. Ramsey's tin of cocaine come back?"

"Not that it's your business, but since Reed's bound to tell you anyway, yes."

"Was it tainted with Veronal?"

A pause was followed by, "How did you know?"

"Beatrice Edgerton's doctor gave her a prescription for Veronal to help her sleep."

"A lot of women are prescribed veronal for sleep disruption."

And men as well, but Ginger left that unsaid. "Mrs. Edgerton believed in poetic justice."

"What kind of justice?"

"Poetic. An ironic twist of fate that feels like deserved retribution."

The superintendent merely grunted in response.

"Please," Ginger pleaded, "just contact Basil and tell him what I've told you. If he hasn't found Howard Pritchard, it's because she has him."

"Because you're Reed's wife, I'll get one of my men to track him down and pass on your message. Will that do?"

Ginger huffed. It would have to. "Thank you, sir."

Basil took a police vehicle so that he could use the bell, which shrilled as he dodged traffic jams and warned distracted pedestrians to get out of his way. Constable Braxton held on to his uniform hat as Basil hurried through busy London streets to the Imperial Institute.

"I'm looking for Howard Pritchard," he said, flashing his metropolitan police identification card. The uniformed officer at his side lent credence to Basil's request for cooperation. "Has anyone seen Mr. Pritchard?"

His pulse raced as he and Braxton scrambled through wide and tall hallways, their footsteps resounding on the marble floors. He scanned the faces of the student body. All Basil wanted to do was arrest his suspect and close this case. He'd promised his friend he would find his son's killer, and that was precisely what he'd done.

"Let's try his room," Basil said. Having been there once before when Pritchard was laid up ill, he knew how to get there quickly. With limber steps and long strides, he came to the door in question and knocked sharply.

"Mr. Pritchard? Police. Open up at once."

"Shall I kick it down?" Constable Braxton offered.

"Not so fast, gentlemen," came the voice of the senior tutor. "No need to get destructive. I have a key."

Basil and Braxton stepped aside until the door swung open. Basil let out a frustrated breath. The room was empty, the bed unmade, and soiled clothing littered the floor. Some fellows didn't have a tidy bone in their bodies, Basil thought. He took a quick look in the wardrobe and under the bed on the off chance that Mr. Pritchard had been tempted to hide, but both spots were empty.

A subsequent visit to the dean garnered no results.

"The students here are quite autonomous," the dean said piously. "Have you enquired with the senior tutor as to Mr. Pritchard's timetable?"

Basil had indeed made the request, and the senior tutor had rushed off to gather the information. Basil turned just as the man reappeared.

"Chief Inspector, he's meant to be in the biology laboratory."

The laboratory was filled with students when Basil and Braxton found it, except for one vacant chair.

"Don't tell me," Basil said. "Mr. Pritchard's place?"

The fellow sitting next to the empty seat replied, "Yes, sir."

Braxton entered quietly and spoke to one of the students who responded with a nod of his head.

Basil was considering his next move when a secretary tracked him down. She was out of breath when she handed him a note.

"A call came in for you from Scotland Yard, sir."

Basil opened the note and swore.

CHAPTER THIRTY-THREE

Ginger hurried to her Crossley, and along with Boss, got in. But instead of driving off, she sat there as if frozen—door opened, unsure of what to do next. She couldn't very well scour the whole city looking for Basil. Frantic desperation swirled in her chest—if she didn't do something quickly, a man would die. But what?

Her thoughts paralysed her, and she nearly jumped through the roof when the sound of tapping resounded on the bonnet. A small fellow with an impish grin stared at her.

"Scout. You scared me half to death."

"Sorry, missus. But, whatcha doin'? Why're ya sittin' in the garage all by yerself?"

Before Ginger could answer, Scout and Boss caught sight of each other.

" 'Ello, boy,"

Ginger gave Scout a look of disapproval, and the boy immediately corrected himself and reinstated the *h.* "I mean h-ello, Boss."

Boss jumped across Ginger's lap, which caused her to let out a sudden breath of air, into Scout's arms and kissed Scout's face. If things hadn't been so dire, Ginger would've enjoyed the moment thoroughly.

Boss wiggled out of Scout's arms and scampered out of the garage. His disappearance was followed by a round of barking.

"What is it, ol' boy?" Scout said chasing after him.

Ginger hesitated. She should be *driving*, but Boss' barking had become incessant, and she couldn't leave without making sure everything was all right. She huffed as she followed the sound.

"Boss?" she called. "Scout?"

"Over 'ere, missus," Scout said. "Boss found sumfing."

Ginger found Boss scratching in the ditch.

"Looks like a fox den, missus. I think I see a pup." Scout quickly added, "Boss won't 'urt 'im," He gathered Boss into his spindly arms. "I promise to 'old 'im back."

Ginger forced a smile. "Go and find Mr. Clement. He'll know what to do."

She watched as the boy and dog ran across the

garden, both of them as happy as clams, then rushed back to the Crossley. She got in and put the machine into reverse. She knew where to go now.

Boss had found a fox den.

A *den of iniquity*.

As quickly as she could, horns blaring about her, and amid shouts of cursing, and near misses, Ginger arrived at Carol Ainsley's studio.

The door to the studio was closed but not locked. Ginger decided to take a chance of encountering a potentially embarrassing situation by not knocking, instead of announcing her arrival to a dangerous one.

In her hand, she held her small silver-plated Remington derringer pistol, a gift from her first husband. There had been times whilst on assignment during the war that Ginger had found herself in heart-pounding situations, sneaking past an enemy, or worse, having to gun one down. Ginger never shot to kill. Why hit the heart when a hip or knee would do?

She'd had the sense to choose soft-soled Italian pumps and lithely approached the sitting room. Through the glass of the French windows, she could see the events unfolding. Howard Pritchard knelt before the coffee table, hands behind his head, whilst Beatrice held the glistening blade of a kitchen knife to Carol's throat. On the table were two rows of white powder.

"Howard, you go first, unless you'd like to see your lover's blood ruin the decor. Don't worry; you'll fall asleep. It's a merciful way to go. More so than what you gave Garrett."

"Mrs. Edgerton, please," Mr. Pritchard pleaded. "It was an accident. I didn't mean for Garrett to die."

"You were like brothers, Howard. You were friends. Yet you held his head underwater until he almost drowned!"

"I was angry. We quarrelled."

Beatrice pressed the blade against Carol's throat. "Over *her*?"

Carol winced as a drop of red ran down the white of her neck.

Howard's eyes darted about like a lamb at the slaughter. "It was stupid, I know, please—"

Ginger inched closer. She had to distract Beatrice enough that she'd loosen her grip on Mrs. Ainsley.

"Tell me, Howard," Beatrice said. "Were you and Bernard under the influence of cocaine when you assaulted my son?"

"Yes. It was the drugs!" Mr. Pritchard's voice pitched upwards as if he might've found a lifeline. "If we hadn't taken the blasted stuff, this wouldn't have happened. We shouldn't have done that. Mrs. Edgerton, I'm frightfully sorry."

Obviously Mr. Pritchard had been overzealous in his claims about not using drugs.

Beatrice's eyes were dull and without sympathy. "And where exactly did you get the dope from?"

Mr. Pritchard's gaze darted to Mrs. Ainsley. She stared steadfastly at the floor.

"Yes, you got it from Carol. Do you know how I know?" Beatrice pushed Carol to her knees. "Because what you're looking at on the table is what I found in the dressing table drawer in this studio. I only added a little something to it. Justice must be served."

Ginger clicked back the hammer of her gun. Beatrice swivelled at the sound, impulsively pointing her weapon at Ginger.

"Mrs. Reed!"

"Mrs. Edgerton."

"What? How? You shouldn't be here."

"And neither should you, I suspect." Ginger held her pistol steady, aiming it back. "Please put the knife down."

"I won't!" Beatrice's hand quivered as she returned the point of the knife to Carol's neck. Her eyes filled with tears. "They stole my son, my only child, from me. They killed him, and now they deserve to die."

"Like Bernard deserved to die?"

"He killed my son!"

"So you killed him and tried to implicate Carol and Howard?" Ginger said.

"A poorly executed plan, I admit," Beatrice said. "Somehow, my Garrett had brought Howard's scarf home, an honest mistake, I'm certain. Carol's awful French cologne was thick on it, and I knew she'd got her claws in him too. I thought the police would put two and two together, but they were too slow. Carol was supposed to go to jail for murder and hang for her crimes, but since the law is bound and determined to fail me, I took matters into my own hands."

"This isn't the way to justice, Beatrice," Ginger said kindly. "Put the knife down and let Mrs. Ainsley go."

Ginger didn't want to shoot the distraught lady, and, thankfully, she wouldn't have to. What Ginger could see from her vantage point, and Beatrice couldn't, was the arrival of Basil and Constable Braxton. Normally, the British police didn't carry weapons, but Basil had a gun. Her urgent message must've driven him to collect one from the Yard's armoury.

They slipped into the sitting room from the kitchen. Basil held his weapon to Beatrice's back and firmly gripped her wrist, easing the blade away from Carol Ainsley's neck.

"It's over, Beatrice," he said. "Give me the knife."

Beatrice stiffened. Her eyes remained on her prey,

but, finally registering defeat, her shoulders slumped. The knife fell from her hand as she loosened her grip and landed with a definitive thud. Her knees weakened, and Basil caught her before she fell to the floor. She sobbed into Basil's chest. "I miss my son, Basil. I miss my son."

It was the saddest thing Ginger had seen in a long, long time.

$\mathcal{G}$inger and Basil snuggled together on the settee in the sitting room—glasses of brandy in their hands and Boss at their feet. Pippins had a nice fire going, and Ginger couldn't help but stare at the Waterhouse mermaid and remember her mother. What would she think about Ginger's pastime of solving crimes?

Howard Pritchard had been arrested for manslaughter, whilst Carol Ainsley, along with the McMillan twins, had been brought up on charges of possession of an illegal substance with the intention of distributing. Mr. Pritchard and Mr. Ramsey had made the unfortunate decision to visit Carol Ainsley the day before the race, each without the knowledge of the other, only to discover that Garrett Edgerton had gone to her first. The fight between the three men hardly upset Mrs. Ainsley, as she'd confessed that her emotions had been subdued by the cocaine she was on.

"Did you see Beatrice today?" Ginger asked.

"Beatrice pleaded guilty to the murder of Bernard Ramsey and to conspiracy to commit murder." Mrs. Edgerton had come to her own conclusion that Mr. Ramsey had killed her son. Perhaps she'd witnessed their altercation at the boathouse that had happened only minutes before Garrett died. She'd let everyone in her household believe she was going to bed, but had instead slipped out of the house and made a visit to Ramsey's room at the student residence. The fact that he wasn't there could've been chance or Beatrice might've assumed he'd gone drinking with Howard Pritchard as the two were seen leaving the Edgerton residence together. At any rate, opportunity presented itself when Beatrice discovered the tin of cocaine which she then laced with her own prescription of Veronal. She was wise enough to keep her gloves on which was why her fingerprints weren't found in the room or on the tin.

"I'm so sorry, love," Ginger said. "Such a tragedy all around, especially for Thurston."

"Yes. Beatrice confessed that she was going to leave Pritchard and Carol Ainsley to die in the manner of the lovers Romeo and Juliet, and then tell the police that she'd found them that way."

"She believed in poetic justice," Ginger said, "however misguided."

"Her solicitor is going to plead insanity derived from a state of unbearable grief."

Ginger's knowledge of the judicial system didn't allow for her to give Beatrice much hope on those grounds, but she nodded.

Her urgent message about Beatrice being after Howard Pritchard had reached Basil, but that wasn't the only message he received. Dr. Gupta had sent word that tests on Garrett's lung tissue showed traces of watercolour paint which pointed to Carol Ainsley and had Basil racing to her studio, which was how he'd come upon Ginger and Beatrice's standoff so quickly.

"There is something else I'd like to tell you about," Ginger said. "There is an office around the corner from Feathers & Flair for let and I want it."

"Whatever for?" Basil asked with sincerity. "You have your study here and the shop at your disposal."

"It would be for my investigative business. I need a place were clients can ring on the telephone or step in off the street. I don't want strangers coming to my home, or into the dress shop. Feathers & Flair has a reputation to sustain and the two sets of clients don't mix."

"I can see your point, love, but just how often do you see yourself investigating for private clients?"

Ginger shrugged. "Who can know that? Besides, manning the telephone will give Felicia something to do beside irritate Madame Roux, and she's always going on about needing a quiet space to write her stories."

"I see you've put a lot of thought into this." Basil didn't look happy or upset, but rather indifferent, which Ginger was pleased to see.

"Yes," she admitted. "You don't mind if I proceed with my plans?"

Basil's lips tugged upwards. "Has anyone ever been able to stop you from getting what you want?"

Ginger patted Basil's arm playfully. "I don't always get what I want, Chief Inspector. The world is too cruel for that."

Basil kissed the top of her head. "Sad, but true, my love."

There was more for them to discuss, but Pippins entered the room just then and announced the arrival of the visitor Ginger was expecting.

"Pippins, you may remain," Ginger said, standing. Then she smiled at a hungry-looking young man.

"Hello, Marvin."

The lad removed his hat and wiped a dirty hand over oily hair. "'Ello, Lady Gold."

"It's Mrs. Reed now. This is my husband, Chief Inspector Reed."

Marvin grew pale and twitched nervously. He nodded, "Sir."

"Please, have a seat, Marvin," Ginger said, hoping the kindness she felt for the lad registered in her eyes.

"I think I'd rather stand, madam."

"You're not in trouble, Marvin. Yes, it's true that we were distraught when you took Scout without permission, but I do understand that you meant him no harm. We've asked you here because we have a proposal for you."

Marvin blinked, his eyes flickering as if he'd just dodged a bullet and wasn't sure how. "Yeah?"

"Scout has been living at Hartigan House for a year, and I hope you can tell that he's healthy and happy here."

"Yes, madam."

"Marvin, the reason I asked you to come tonight is because I would like to offer you an opportunity to serve your country as part of the Royal Navy." Ginger had pulled some strings and agreed to take financial responsibility for Marvin Elliot. "You would be well looked after, with good meals, a warm bed, and be given training. You'd never have to scrape by on the streets again, and you'd make social retribution for the crimes you once committed."

"Would I ever see Scout again?" Ginger

empathised with Marvin. He truly loved his little cousin.

"Of course. You can stay with us whenever you have leave."

Marvin's pale face regained colour. "I would be in your debt, Mrs. Reed. I don't know how I can repay your kindness to me and Scout."

"You may stay the night in the servants' quarters. I've already arranged it with Pippins. A taxicab will collect you in the morning and deliver you to Waterloo Station where you will then take a train to Portsmouth Harbour."

"Thank you, madam." He bowed to Basil saying, "Sir," and then followed Pippins out of the room.

Ginger found her way back into the crook of Basil's arm.

"That felt good. Fate has brought these two children into my life, our life, and Marvin is part of us."

Ginger felt Basil's mouth as he kissed her head.

"Your heart is as big as the sea, my love."

"Sometimes, it does feel as if it will burst."

"There is something more we need to talk about," Basil said. There was a note of trepidation in his voice.

"About Scout?" Ginger answered quickly, hoping that their adoption prospect was what Basil was referring to.

"It's not about Scout," Basil said, "though you're

right. We need to have a good discussion about that soon."

Ginger closed her eyes. "It's about my taking Beatrice on as a client and not telling you, isn't it?"

"Yes."

Ginger faced her husband. She'd never tire of looking at those hazel eyes, though it hurt her to see that they were registering disappointment.

"Why didn't you tell me?"

"I wanted to, Basil, but she made me promise, and I had to honour her wishes. Besides, things wouldn't have turned out any differently if I had. And when we married, you understood that I would continue running my businesses, and that includes Lady Gold Investigations."

"It seems rather unfair that you expect me to bring you into my investigations, whilst you keep me out of yours."

"You're right. I should've said no to Beatrice, and I was going to, but she was so sad about Garrett, I just didn't have the heart."

Basil wrapped his arms around Ginger, and she pushed closer. "I want to continue working as your consultant, Basil. I'm good at it. You know I am."

"Indeed, you are. Can we agree that we shall work as each other's consultant? That way, we won't inadvertently undermine one another's investigations or put the other in harm's way."

"I can agree to that, Mr. Reed."

"In that case," Basil said with a hint of a tease, "I think we need to seal the deal." He reached for Ginger's chin.

"Consider it sealed," she said, then settled her lips on his.

The End

Read on for more from LA PLUME PRESS

If you enjoyed reading *Murder at the Boat Club* please help others enjoy it too.

Recommend it: Help others find the book by recommending it to friends, readers' groups, discussion boards and by **suggesting it to your local library.**

Review it: Please tell other readers why you liked this book by reviewing it on Amazon or Goodreads.

Introducing LADY GOLD INVESTIGATES!

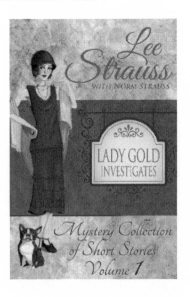

Ginger Gold has opened her own private investigation office!

This short story companion series to Ginger Gold Mysteries has the clever Mrs. Ginger Reed, aka Lady Gold, and her adventurous sister-in-law Felicia taking on clients who've got all sorts of troubles. This first volume consists of *The Case of the Wayward Wife*, and *The Case of the Boy who Vanished*.

A companion series to Ginger Gold Mysteries, each volume is approximately 20 thousand words or 80 pages. A bite size read perfect for a transit commute home, time spent waiting at an appointment, or to settle into sleep at night. Get your coffee, tea or glass of wine and snuggle in!

ON AMAZON

Don't miss MURDER ON EATON SQUARE
Ginger Gold Book # 10

Murder's Bad Karma. . .

Life couldn't be better on Eaton Square

Gardens where the most prestigious families lived, until one of their own dies and it's *murder*.

Ginger and Basil are on the case, but it's not a simple glass of bubbly fizz. The more the clues present themselves, the trickier the puzzle gets, and Ginger feels she's on a wild goose chase.

But as someone close to the victim so aptly quips, "One shouldn't commit murder. It's bad karma."

Reaping what one sows is hardly a great cup of tea.

Read on Amazon
or order from your favorite bookstore.

Introducing LADY GOLD INVESTIGATES!

Ginger Gold has opened her own private investigation office!

This short story companion series to Ginger Gold Mysteries has the clever Mrs. Ginger Reed, aka Lady Gold, and her adventurous sister-in-law Felicia taking on clients who've got all sorts of troubles. This first volume consists of *The Case of the Wayward Wife,* and *The Case of the Boy who Vanished.*

A companion series to Ginger Gold Mysteries, each volume is approximately 20 thousand words or 80 pages. A bite size read perfect for a transit commute home, time spent waiting at an appointment, or to settle into sleep at night. Get your coffee, tea or glass of wine and snuggle in!

ON AMAZON
or order from your favorite bookstore.

GINGER GOLD'S JOURNAL

Sign up for Lee's readers list and gain access to **Ginger Gold's private Journal.** Find out about Ginger's Life before the SS *Rosa* and how she became the woman she has. This is a fluid document that will cover her romance with her late husband Daniel, her time serving in the British secret service during World War One, and beyond. Includes a recipe for Dark Dutch Chocolate Cake!

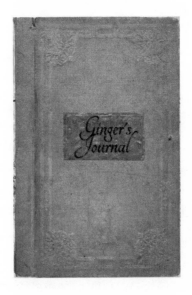

It begins: **July 31, 1912**

How fabulous that I found this Journal today, hidden in the bottom of my wardrobe. Good old Pippins, our English butler in London, gave it to me as a parting gift when Father whisked me away on our American adventure so he could marry Sally. Pips said it was for me to record my new adventures. I'm ashamed I never even penned one word before today. I think I was just too sad.

This old leather-bound journal takes me back to that emotional time. I had shed enough tears to fill the ocean and I remember telling

Father dramatically that I was certain to cause flooding to match God's. At eight years old I was well-trained in my biblical studies, though, in retro-spect, I would say that I had probably bordered on heresy with my little tantrum.

The first week of my "adventure" was spent with a tummy ache and a number of embarrassing sessions that involved a bucket and Father holding back my long hair so I wouldn't soil it with vomit.

I certainly felt that I was being punished for some reason. Hartigan House—though large and sometimes lonely—was my home and Pips was my good friend. He often helped me to pass the time with games of I Spy and Xs and Os.

"Very good, Little Miss," he'd say with a twinkle in his blue eyes when I won, which I did often. I suspect now that our good butler wasn't beyond letting me win even when unmerited.

Father had got it into his silly head that I needed a mother, but I think the truth was he wanted a wife. Sally, a woman half my father's age, turned out to be a sufficient wife in the end, but I could never claim her as a mother.

Well, Pips, I'm sure you'd be happy to know that things turned out all right here in America.

Go to leestraussbooks.com to learn more.

.

LADY GOLD INVESTIGATES (Ginger Gold companion short stories)

Volume 1

Volume 2

Volume 3

HIGGINS & HAWKE MYSTERY SERIES (cozy 1930s historical)

The 1930s meets Rizzoli & Isles in this friendship depression era cozy mystery series.

Death at the Tavern

Death on the Tower

Death on Hanover

A NURSERY RHYME MYSTERY SERIES (mystery/sci fi)

Marlow finds himself teamed up with intelligent and savvy Sage Farrell, a girl so far out of his league he feels blinded in her presence - literally - damned glasses! Together they work to find the identity of @gingerbreadman. Can they stop the killer before he strikes again?

Gingerbread Man

Life Is but a Dream

Hickory Dickory Dock

Twinkle Little Star

THE PERCEPTION TRILOGY (YA dystopian mystery)

Zoe Vanderveen is a GAP—a genetically altered person. She lives in the security of a walled city on prime water-front property along side other equally beautiful people with extended life spans. Her brother Liam is missing. Noah Brody, a boy on the outside, is the only one who can help ∼ but can she trust him?

Perception

Volition

Contrition

LIGHT & LOVE (sweet romance)

Set in the dazzling charm of Europe, follow Katja, Gabriella, Eva, Anna and Belle as they find strength, hope and love.

Sing me a Love Song

Your Love is Sweet

In Light of Us

Lying in Starlight

PLAYING WITH MATCHES (WW2

history/romance)

A sobering but hopeful journey about how one young Germany boy copes with the war and propaganda. Based on true events.

A Piece of Blue String (companion short story)

THE CLOCKWISE COLLECTION (YA time travel romance)

Casey Donovan has issues: hair, height and uncontrollable trips to the 19th century! And now this ∼ she's accidentally taken Nate Mackenzie, the cutest boy in the school, back in time. Awkward.

Clockwise

Clockwiser

Like Clockwork

Counter Clockwise

Clockwork Crazy

Clocked (companion novella)

Standalones

As Elle Lee Strauss

Seaweed

Love, Tink

ABOUT THE AUTHOR

Lee Strauss is a USA TODAY bestselling author of The Ginger Gold Mysteries series, The Higgins & Hawke Mystery series (cozy historical mysteries), A Nursery Rhyme Mystery series (mystery suspense), The Perception series (young adult dystopian), The Light & Love series (sweet romance), The Clockwise Collection (YA time travel romance), and young adult historical fiction with over a million books read. She has titles published in German, Spanish and Korean, and a growing audio library.

When Lee's not writing or reading she likes to cycle, hike, and play pickleball. She loves to drink caffè lattes and red wines in exotic places, and eat dark chocolate anywhere.

For more info on books by Lee Strauss and her social media links, visit leestraussbooks.com. To make sure you don't miss the next new release, be sure to sign up for her readers' list!

Did you know you can follow your favourite authors on Bookbub? If you subscribe to Bookbub — (and if you don't, why don't you? - They'll send you daily emails alerting you to sales and new releases on just the kind of books you like to read!) — follow me to make sure you don't miss the next Ginger Gold Mystery!

www.leestraussbooks.com

leestraussbooks@gmail.com